Bella

An Appalachian Love Story

&

Jagged Dawn

Logan's Beginning

Bella: An Appalachian Love Story & Jagged Dawn: Logan's Beginning

By Valerie Davisson

Bella: An Appalachian Love Story & Jagged Dawn: Logan's Beginning are works of fiction. Names, characters, places, and incidents are the product of the author's imagination or are used fictitiously. Any resemblance to actual events, locales, businesses, or persons, living or dead, is coincidental.

Published by Vaughn House Publishing, Depoe Bay, OR
Second Edition

Print ISBN - 978-1-7340119-3-7
Ebook ISBN - 978-1-7340119-4-4

Cover and Interior Design by Kimberly Peticolas, www.kimpeticolas.com

Library of Congress Control Number: 2020905580

10 9 8 7 6 5 4 3 2 1

Bella

An Appalachian Love Story

&

Jagged Dawn

Logan's Beginning

VALERIE DAVISSON

Bella

An Appalachian Love Story

To my loyal readers, new readers, and anyone who has ever come up to me at a book fair, sent me an email, or stopped me in the grocery store to tell me how much they enjoyed one of my books. Thank you for allowing me to continue doing what I love.

This one's for you!

Chapter One

1966
RED SLEEVE, WV

Norah

" **J**ust start anywhere, Grandma. I want to know everything," Will said.

"Well, then, get comfortable. I'll start with George. It was mid-summer when I first saw him leanin' against the outside of the church house. Sally told me that young man was Beulah's cousin, come to help her daddy clear the land that rose behind their cabin about halfway up the holler. George was a few inches shorter than most of the boys 'round here, and weighed half as much, but I noticed him right away, though I didn't let on.

"They were fixin' to put in more corn. It was hard work. Too hard for her daddy, who'd cut his leg up last winter and never got the full use of it back. Mountain trees don't give up their roots easy. More rocks than dirt mostly on that mountain, but they needed to clear more land. Beulah's mom had seven mouths to feed. At fourteen, Beulah was the oldest.

"Not me. I was the onliest child at our place—a thing almost unheard of in the holler. Everybody had near twelve to twenty children back then. But my Mommy and Poppy drowned in the flood back '09 before they could make me any brothers or sisters. Grandpa Harley & Granny Louise, who I'm named after—well, my middle name—took and raised me up. Grandpa mostly.

"Granny took sick and died two years afore, when I was twelve. Still, she taught me most what I needed to know to take care of Grandpa and me. I could make good lye soap, get up a basket out of white oak splits, plant by the signs, put up runner beans and tomatoes for the winter. And berries. We had a mess of blackberries every year. We had chickens and a hog. What we didn't grow or make ourselves, we traded for with our neighbors.

"It was Grandpa Harley and Granny Louise's sister, Aunt Leila, what taught me the two things I really loved, though, and done me the most good in this life. Medicine and music. And stories. They both could spin a yarn.

"Nearest doctor was a day's ride by horseback and nobody we knew even owned a horse, just a mule if they were lucky. Aunt Leila was our doctor. She didn't have a husband or children, so she spent more time learnin' how to help other folks with theirs. And she did. Herbs, poultices, potions. She could fix or cure most anything: broke bones, burns, whoopin' cough or mountain fever. And what she couldn't cure, she'd soothe just by bein' there with 'em. Pray with 'em if they were believers. Sometimes that's all you can do, she'd tell me—just ease a person's sufferin'. She knew that. The love in her heart was as powerful as the herbs she gathered, the potions she mixed up, or the poultices in her larder.

"I didn't take to the prayer part. It seemed to me God helped those that helped themselves. He put the plants and such there for us and it was our job to use the brain he gave us to figure out how to use them. Prayer had nothin' to do with it. Leastwise it didn't save Granny Louise. I tried.

"Grandpa Harley gave me music. People came from three, four hollers away to hear him fiddle. He was so good. I can't remember a night without the sweet sounds he could coax out of a few pieces of wood and string. Lightnin' fast for dances and weddings and long, Scottish wails and lullabies on summer nights playin' on the porch for the crickets. He once told me that to him music was food—as fillin' as Granny Louise's buttermilk biscuits and just as essential. Give you life. Or at least make it worth livin'.

"I felt the same way. And it's a good thing because we went without biscuits of any kind until I learned not to burn 'em after Granny died. I'd watch Grandpa's fingers fly so fast I couldn't see where they went and how at other times he pulled the bow across the strings real slow, his eyes closed tight, to make a longing, sad sound like you never heard. It would set my heart to thrumming. I could sit for hours and listen to him play. I especially liked it when a thunderstorm would roll down the mountain to back him up. He'd be silhouetted against the black rain clouds and the wind would whip up his hair—the little bit he had left that is. He'd play until the cold would make us come inside.

"Sometimes, when he was out choppin' wood, I'd take his violin down and try to copy what I'd seen him do. The first time I did it, Grandpa came a runnin', said I liked to scared him to death. Said he thought a wildcat had got to me with all that screeching. He pretended to be mad, but I knew he wasn't. He said as long as I was gonna mess around with it, I might as well learn to play it right. He showed me to tuck it under my chin and how to hold my arm up like a bird's wing. I got better.

"Grandpa made me this here ladder-back chair so's I could sit up straight on the edge of it when I played. I never had no dolls. Didn't want any either, as long as I could fiddle or wander the hills with Aunt Leila, huntin' up roots an' plants or mushrooms.

"Finally, Grandpa told me he was tired of me hoggin' his. Said I needed to get my own fiddle. I thought I'd die. I knew such a thing cost upwards to seven or eight dollars in the Sears Roebuck catalogue. That don't seem like much now—specially up in the city where you're from—but it was as high as the moon back then. Way out of my reach. I didn't have no money and no way of makin' any. I don't know how he put up with my hangdog ways that summer, but he kept a poker face on him for weeks. One night after the sun went down—I think it must have been late August—Aunt Leila come over one night and made a fine dinner. Hambone and beans, greens, and cornbread to sop up the juice. It was one of my favorite dinners, but I hardly ate a bite.

"But then she pulled somethin' out of her big bag. I couldn't believe my eyes! It was a case that could only hold a violin. She placed it in my hands. Said it was from her and Grandpa both. She didn't say how, but she must have saved money up from her birthin' trips—she was also the best midwife for miles around. Grandpa must have had a few coins saved, too. They ordered me my very own genuine Stradivarius Model violin from the Sears, Roebuck & Co catalogue. Of course, it was just a cheap thing with a fancy name, but I didn't care. I thought my violin was beautiful! Curly maple back and sides. The kit came with a case, a songbook, and a full set of strings. That summer, I neglected all but my most important chores until I was good enough to play with Grandpa at dances and weddings. My fiddle never did sound as good as Grandpa's— he got his off'n a German family movin' west; it came from the old country where they knew how to make them.

Bella

"I wish I could give you those hours, those pine-filled nights on the porch, lightnin' bugs dancin' in the growin' night, the air still soft with summer, but with fall's sharp edge to it, stomachs full, washing up done, wood stove stoked, and Grandpa and me playin' up the moon while Aunt Leila rocked content, smokin' her pipe.

"But I was talkin' about George, wasn't I? Hard to keep the tellin' on a straight path. There's so much to tell."

Chapter Two

MANTUA, ITALY

In the summer of 1881, Tomasso Morandi, baker's certificate in hand, along with his good friends, Micheli Basso, a newly-minted luthier, or violin maker, and Mauro, a young man of no discernible talents other than telling tall tales, left their native city, Cremona, and moved to the Northern Italian town of Mantua, seventy kilometers away. Cremona had only boring views of the immensely flat, agricultural Padana plain out of every window, while Mantua was a multi-faceted jewel nestled among three sparkling lakes. An up-and-coming economic and cultural center in the area, it held the excitement and opportunity the young men craved.

Micheli, working out of a couple of small rooms in town, immediately began competing with other luthiers in making the beautiful violins for which the city was becoming famous. Even Mauro found his way. While staying with Micheli, Mauro would stack the chunks of wood the artisan had rejected for not having the sound quality necessary to be made into musical instruments. Eventually, he began to notice how the grain ran through certain pieces and how particularly interesting knots or other discrepancies reminded him of eyes or ears. In the firelight they moved and

11

danced, entering his dreams. Within a week he had carved his first puppet and within a month had carved and painted a full cast, which he took on the road telling his stories in an ever-evolving puppet show to cities and towns all over Italy, eventually finding a home for his marionettes in Venice.

Sinking his roots deeply into the soil of his new home, Tomasso Morandi quickly married the prettiest girl in town and became Tomasso da Mantua, establishing himself as one of the most popular, if not the most important, men in the region. A lover of food, family, and wine—and all things pleasurable—Tomasso was perfectly suited to life in a town named after the Etruscan god Mantus—even if that god ruled the underworld. In time, they had five sons and two daughters. Then, four years after the last of the seven was born, his wife gave birth to their eighth child—a son they named Giovanni.

o o o o o

1924
ABOARD THE ST. MICHELE
GENOA TO NEW YORK
STEERAGE

Giovanni De Mantua

"I come from the north, from a town called Mantua, many miles from your home," Giovanni began, as he sat with Lorenzo aboard the ship headed to New York. "Mantua is a special place. I expected to live there, near my family, for the rest of my life. But, obviously, since I am here on this ship with you that did not happen.

"Everyone came to my father's *panetteria*! I can still remember the heavenly smells wafting through the narrow streets every morning, pulling the people toward the piazza, which filled with market stands each day. It was a good life he made for us there. We were happy and no one went hungry in Mantua, as I know many people did in the south."

Lorenzo nodded knowingly. He and his family had left southern Italy for that very reason.

"I am sorry—you are from Sicily," Giovanni said, "It must have been very hard there."

"Yes, it is still very hard," he said, "that is why we are here with you on this ship. But let us not be sad tonight! Share a meal with us and tell me more of this place, your home, and why you would leave such a wonderful place. I have heard it sparkled and never ran out of water! We hope to find such places in America, where I can farm. We have a long journey before us, the children are sleeping, so your story will help pass the time."

"You are right about the city. Every corner of Mantua held not only nourishment for the body, but for the spirit also. The palazzo no longer housed a royal family, but since the unification of Italy, it was open to all. And what treasures it held! Greek and Roman sculptures, paintings by Ruben, and Flemish tapestries. The gardens in the *Corte Vecchia* delighted the eye. And music! Verdi, Puccini . . . as you know, opera holds a special place in every Italian's heart.

"But the violin, it was the violin that captured my soul. It was the sound each violin made, its particular voice, I found fascinating. I wanted to know how to create these delicate yet strong instruments. I often went with my father to visit his friend, violin artisan Micheli Basso, in his shop at the other end of the piazza, down a quiet street. He wasn't the only luthier in Mantua—there were many—but he was the best.

"His shop was a magical place that was filled with the smells of wood and varnish, sweat and leather, and the sounds of knocking and scraping. Always the sounds of scrapping, chipping bits of wood away until the perfect form was achieved. And men. Men and boys curved over their work, behind walls hung with all manner of tools I could not comprehend, all focused on doing their best to create the perfect form to release the purest sound from the wood. Golden light poured through the front windows, bathing the violins on display in a warm glow. Some of the instruments seemed almost alive, so beautifully were they created.

"Rejecting the thick and showy paints of the modern violin makers, Basso's slender violins kept to the traditions of the classics, so after a year of begging and with the flow of coins my father earned as a successful baker, it was to this master of masters I was apprenticed at the age of eleven. I would complete a few years of schooling first, then finish my training in the shop. I would learn at the master's knee, or so I thought, and he would be the only arbiter of my fate, the one who would send me out into the world as soon as I had earned the right to open my own shop by passing the test of creating a well-crafted violin. But all of this would require many years of exacting training first. I didn't mind. I wanted to be the best."

Chapter Three

Giovanni

"My brothers had all been apprenticed already. I was the youngest and therefore was kept to help my father in the bakery as long as possible. But it was clear I did not have natural talent as he did for bringing flour and sugar to life, so he cheerfully relented and let me go. My oldest brother was being trained to take over the bakery, so when our father became unable to do the heavy, physical labor required, all would remain in the family.

"As with most things, the view from the inside of the violin shop was very different from the view of a visitor. As a guest, and the son of one of his best friends, the Master Basso always had a kind word and often a treat for me when I visited—a toy he or one of the men in the shop had fashioned for me from a bit of wood or string. Once, he pulled a tiny, orange kitten out of one of his large, square coat pockets.

"Good for catching rats," he informed my father, winking at me. I named her Duchessa, as she quickly ruled the bakery kitchen with her imperious ways.

"I played on the floor while they talked above me. We never stayed long. Both men were busy.

"But once I started my apprenticeship, I occupied a small room at the back of the master's house—all apprentices lived with the master's family. I did not see him smile as often then, at least not in my direction. I ate at their table, but his smiles were reserved for his wife, Signora Basso, a kind and beautiful woman, and his son, Antonio. Now that I was his apprentice, my role was a more serious one. Several years later when I had completed my formal schooling, I could now work in the shop full time. I was about fourteen and hungry to learn.

"I remember that first morning. The street was quiet, shutters still closed against the cold. Master Basso walked purposefully, along the lake, then turned down a curving street. He carried a thick piece of wood under his arm—about the size of a large log for the fire. His steps rang out on the cold stone street. My small ones tapped behind his. I never did learn where this piece of wood came from—most of the wood he used was stored on open shelves in the back of his shop, to air-dry and age, sometimes over many years.

"He placed this one with reverence on his workbench once inside the shop. Reaching up, he removed his work coat from the hook by the door and pulled it on, buttoning it against the chill. He looked at the wood, then unrolled and studied the parchment patterns he kept in a drawer. I watched, fascinated.

"With the first knuckle on his left hand, he tapped the wood and listened intently to the tone. A smile hovered on his lips. Totally focused on the wood, it was as if I were invisible. I felt privileged to watch him work when no one else was yet in the shop. I held my breath.

"First, he pulled down a saw and divided the log into equal halves, then even boards. Holding two pieces up next to each other, he tapped them again with a mallet of his own design. Satisfied, he took a deep breath and I took the chance to breath quietly in rhythm with him.

"Next, he reached for a brush. Dipping it into a pot of thick, black glue, he fastened the pieces together. Later, he would trace the ancient pattern onto the wood and cut out the well-known shape of a violin, which reminded me of Signora Basso's curves, though I knew not to say so aloud.

"Over the years, I watched many times as he went through the same exacting steps to make a violin. It only took a couple of weeks to construct one, but the finishing and varnishing took much longer, so the whole process for one violin might take three to six months.

"Patiently, over the next few days, he scraped away the excess wood until he had the perfect thickness in each area, hollowing out the center, which would later hold what he called the voice of God. With great precision, he carved and tapped in the inlay around the edges. He had gauges and tools and ways of measuring, but he had the gift—this knowing of what to take away and what to leave.

"And when the body was complete, finely sanded and finished, it was still not done. Considering the many glass bottles and containers of different shapes and sizes on his shelves, the master selected this one and that one, scraping something off this small block with his knife, crushing this element into that liquid, dipping and swabbing samples until he was satisfied. Then, with great care, as if stroking a lover, he rubbed the varnish into the wood to bring out its grain and beauty. Many drying and curing periods came between these stages. He sometimes applied as many as forty coats of varnish, finely drying and sanding each one before applying the next.

"Finally, when he was satisfied, he hung the completed

violin on the wall, glinting demurely for all to see. Two doves sat in the window cooing their approval and I vowed to make something just as beautiful one day."

Chapter Four

Giovanni

"Please, go on! The wine is of our region from my uncle's vineyard," Lorenzo said.

"Well, when I was fifteen, I graduated from sweeping up and running errands to learning how to make every part of a violin. All I needed now was more practice. The final step to completing my apprenticeship and earn my certificate was to make an instrument completely on my own, fine enough to pass Master Basso's rigorous standards. It was to this end I dedicated my every waking hour. It was 1916 and many apprentices already had their certificates. Competition was fierce.

"As a young man, I had, of course, noticed the young girls in the city, and assumed someday to marry as my father had, but I did not permit myself to even linger near, let alone speak with any one girl. There was no point in going further, even in my thoughts. My first priority was to get that certificate, set up a shop for myself and begin earning enough to support a family. Only then would any woman's father permit me to see her.

"So, for the next few years, I continued to work hard and focus on refining my skills, not joining Antonio and his friends when they went out drinking and gambling. Besides, as an apprentice, although I had food and a safe place to sleep, I had little money of my own.

"It was about this time that the master's own skills began to decline. He developed a slight tremor in his hands which I could tell upset him greatly, but it was his hearing, I think, that worried him most. To add to his anxiety, business had slowed as showier violins became more popular and the fame of the city continued to attract more and more violin makers, making it harder to make a living, no matter your skill.

"Eventually, from a once thriving shop with nine apprentices, we were down to just two, myself and the master's son, Antonio. Antonio was about my age, but did not have his father's natural gifts. Barely competent, he was only there because he was his father's only son, and everyone knew it, including Antonio.

"What the master was losing was his 'ear', the ability to hear the ringing tone necessary to select the best pieces of wood for the construction of the most melodious violins. He would purchase small lots of promising wood, preferably aged, and then go through them as he had time—keeping some, using the rejected logs for furniture or firewood. Formerly, he would perform this important task himself, but as he progressively could not trust his own hearing, and knowing Antonio was less than useless at this task, he would ask me to do it. I had the gift!

"Not directly of course, he always put it as part of my training. His hearing was still good enough to narrow it down to several pieces of wood first. Then he would send Antonio away on some errand or wait until the end of the day, sending his son home and asking me to stay and clean up the shop. As soon as Antonio left, he would put me to the test, having me knock each piece of wood with the first knuckle of the middle finger of my left hand. If any of them resounded with that strong, ringing tone, I would hold it up. He would then nod and instruct me to place it in the rack to be used to make the next violin for his best customers, those he would craft himself.

"Antonio was not a fool. As his father's hand tremors increased and he asked for my assistance more often and openly, the tension between Antonio and me grew. Knowing my position would never be as strong as a son's natural one, I had always taken great care not to flaunt my skill or give him any reason to resent me more than he already did. But I don't think anything I did could have prevented what happened."

"What happened?" Giovanni's new friends asked.

"Nothing, right away. One winter morning, a Signor Valerio, a well-known patron of the arts in Mantua, entered the shop, requesting a violin be made for a promising young musician he wanted to encourage, and in time for the city music festival at the end of the summer. The violin was to be of the best materials, made in the traditional way, and could only be trusted to Master Basso, of course! Time was of the essence and cost was of little concern.

"To satisfy such an important customer would mean Master Basso's name would be spoken in the salons of the wealthy men in town. It would also restore and secure his reputation as the best luthier in Mantua. This was a very important job.

"Forgetting to send Antonio on an errand in his excitement, Master Basso directed me to follow him to the back of the shop. Antonio's eyes followed, but he stayed where he was and said nothing. The master had me knocking on almost every wedge of wood he had in the storage room—which had been aging anywhere from two months to two decades—not even bothering to pretend to test me so eager was he to begin this new project. He had me select the most beautifully resonant piece.

"We worked for several hours. We were about to stop for the night and go home to one of Signora Basso's excellent meals when I pulled two pieces out from one of the bottom shelves. Both were excellent. One had a slightly fuller tone than the other, but either would make a very fine instrument for Signor Valerio's violinist. Finally, choosing the piece with the fuller tone, I placed the first one back on the pile and held the chosen piece up for him to see and hear. Pleased, he clasped me by the shoulders and smiled widely in approval.

"Picking up the second best piece of wood, he held it out to me with these words, "When you have completed your current work, you begin work on your own violin! This piece should be worthy of your efforts.

"Laughing at the expression on my face, he clapped me on the back, embraced me, and then began striding to the front of the shop, with me in tow."

Chapter Five

1966
RED SLEEVE, WV

Norah

"George was quiet, like he had secrets to share, but not the need to do so. They said he was a hard worker. Beyond that, the normal curiosity folks had didn't apply. He was only there for the summer. Come fall, once the patch of land was cleared, he'd be leavin' Red Sleeve, goin' back to Gallville, about an hour south. There were coal minin' jobs there. Even with the trouble the year before in Mattewan, men still went down into the mines. It was the only job a man could get in these parts.

"Every week, when church let out, I'd see George there, leanin' against the porch railin' in the same spot, smokin'. All by hisself. He was near a man, comin' up on eighteen, older than most of the local boys trying to court me. I never spoke to him, but I forced myself not to hurry down the stairs when I walked past, neither. I'd take my time sayin' goodbye to Sally, then finally take off on my own, followin' Willow Creek up to our cabin. I could feel that boy's eyes on me until I was out of sight, but I never looked back over my shoulder.

"I got myself to church and back. Grandpa didn't go. Later in my life, I didn't either, but back then, it was just somethin' everyone did. We lived the farthest up the holler, which suited Grandpa and me just fine. Besides the church, the blacksmith, and the general store, there wasn't much else there. Folks got mail there, and bought what they couldn't borrow or trade when they had money.

"Finally, one Sunday, I hung back until most everyone left. I peeked out the window and saw George was still there, waitin'. I took a chance and looked up at him as I walked out the church door and headed down those stairs. He tipped his hat and asked me sideways, lookin' straight out to the road so as not to be embarrassed if I said no, if he could walk me home. I allowed as he could and from then on, everyone knew we were courtin'. Other boys had asked, but I'd always said no.

"Grandpa'd been holdin' off makin' a match for me, even though I was already sixteen and most of my friends were married and had one or two younguns. I didn't want to marry, but I knew it was time I lived the life of a woman, not a child. I liked George and had the feelings a girl has for a boy, but I seen what a woman's life was. I was in none too big a hurry to take that up. I'd been to birthings with Aunt Leila, and was scared to death of bein' ripped that way, or dyin'.

"But that's the natural way of things and I didn't have no say, anyhow.

"Not long after they got the hay in and it was spread to dry, Grandpa got the preacher to come, who was also a magistrate. Aunt Leila fixed up my best blue serge dress, George borrowed his cousin's suit and slicked his hair back. Preacher had a funeral to get to in the next holler, so people were still comin' in when he gathered us on the porch.

Bella

"For as much as Joseph George McKenna and Nora Louise Glenn have consented together in wedlock, and have witnessed the same before this company of friends and family, and have given and pledged their promises to each other. By the authority vested in me by the State of West Virginia, I pronounce this couple to be husband and wife. What God hath joined together, let no man put asunder."

—Magistrate Asgood
August 1921

"He left out the part about the rings, 'cause we didn't have none. Most young folks couldn't afford rings at that time. With that, the preacher hurried off so as to have the light. Whole thing didn't take more'n five minutes. And then I was a married woman. I didn't feel much different 'til later.

"As with most mountain weddings, the whole holler came. Ever'body liked to show their specialty at a potluck. We had scrapple, hog's head stew, ribs, beans, sweet-cakes, chowchow, grits, greens, and of course, a jar or two got passed around out back of Levi's special shine. And so many pies. But my favorite was the stack cake. Everyone brought a layer of dried apple cake and I was proud mine towered up twelve layers high!

"You know about shivarees? Just somethin' silly mountain boys do. Some call 'em serenades. Didn't rough George up too much, though, then delivered him back to the cabin all of a-piece. We didn't have our own place, so Grandpa ran a line cross't the back of the cabin and hung a blanket over it. Aunt Leila fixed it up nice. Freshened up the tickin' and when they brought George back and we said our good nights, the first thing I saw was a fine weddin' ring quilt spread across my marriage bed. So, we didn't need the rings anyhow. Made it official. I didn't know it, but she'd made that top a while back. She know'd I'd marry someday. When she saw which way the wind was blowin' with George and me, she got some muslin and a thicker layer to put between, and the women quilted it all together. I'd never had anything that nice. Those women could make the tiniest stitches. Mine were never that fine.

"Had to leave it behind when I left Gallville. Barely made it out with my fiddle and the clothes on my back . . . and Elsie."

Chapter Six

Norah

"*If you got a mule killed in the mines, you could lose your job over it. If you got a man killed, he could be replaced.*"

—*Terry Steele*
Coal Miner and proud member of the local UMWA

"Our new home was only an hour away, but I'd never been that far away before. Gallville might just have been on the dark side of the moon. Never seen nothin' like it. Never been to a minin' town before. I wondered if they all looked like this one. One straight stretch of muddy road ran right up the middle, 'longside the railroad track, lined with sigogglin crackerboxes all cheek and jowl together. But the strangest part, the part that hit my eye right off, was the grey of it. Not a bit o' green anywheres. No trees, no bushes. Even the sound had no color. No birdsong. No children laughin'. And everything thick with coal dust, like a mean fairy'd been through and sprinkled everything different shades o' black.

"Made our home in the holler—the one we're sittin' in here—seem like a palace. Grandpa cut the logs for this place, notched and planed and fit them all together to make it good and tight against the weather for Granny Louise. They raised up their children and then me after Mommy and Poppy died. And it's still a standin'. I expect it'll be standin' a good long while more.

"Lookin' at those shacks, I didn't understand why the mine would want to make a house that'd blow down in a strong wind. But that's just what those mine owners did. Didn't make 'em strong to last 'cause they knew the coal'd run out eventually and when it did, they'd just close down the town and make another whole town where the coal was.

Will shook his head in wonder as he looked around her house. "I love this place. It's so peaceful here. Nothing like back home."

"Yes, it's beautiful here. Oh, I know you think you'd like to live here, but you're a city boy—you wouldn't know the first thing about livin' back up here. Now, don't get all bent outta shape. Course you can stay here for the rest of the summer, but come the first freeze, you need to get yourself back to school. Education. That's what you need now to live in the outside world. No offense, but you don't got the skills to live here. These skills is only good for livin' here. Every place has its way. You got to learn the ways of your place. It's nice now, in the summer, but come winter . . . winter's long, boy. It can get lonely. It's the only life I know, so it's good for me.

"But, back to my story.

"George promised me a house, too, and so, even though the one they give us in Gallville wasn't much more than a few thin boards slapped together with a wobbly porch out front, I tried to act pleased. It was 1922, so's we had 'lectricity. George was so proud, but there was just one drop light hangin' down on the porch.

"They give us coal for free, Norah!" he told me.

"I don't know who he was tryin' to convince, him or me.

"We soon learned nothin' was for free in that town. I grew what I could once spring came, but we had to buy most everything through the winter at the company store, and the prices were high. It was all taken out of George's pay, and when there wasn't enough, they either turned you away or run you an 'account' which you could never pay off. Least wise I never heard anyone did.

"As bad as things were, we were still better off than some. Grandpa give us some salt pork, a bag of dried beans, some taters, and some lard in a gallon jar. Packed a tote sack with a little of everything from the garden we'd did and put away. Aunt Leila made me up a bundle of dried herbs—balm of Gilead and such. George's people loaned us a mule for the trip and we packed her up. We walked, each of us loaded up 'bout near as much as the mule. But I was glad I had what I had when I got there. George's sister, who lived at the end of the row, had five or six chill-uns and nary a pot to pee in.

"It hurt me to see the little ones so rail thin and raggedy. I thought of all the sacks of sweet potatoes, apples, corn, okra, and leather breeches beans, leanin' on the walls back home. Cabbages and onions dug in and piled up on each other and covered in straw. We traded those for Marley's honey. Fresh eggs, chickens, and most everybody kept a hog or even two.

"That winter I gave away what food we could spare, and took to doctorin' other women's children with what I remembered from what Aunt Leila taught me. People just started showin' up at my door. I'd help 'em with what I had, then come spring when we could finally put in a small garden, the fresh greens helped those children more than anything.

"Life in Gallville had a different rhythm than life in the holler. The days had a sameness to 'em, not like back home. Back home, things changed natural, along with the sun, the moon, rain, and stars. People planted by the signs. The signs even helps you know when to dig a post hole or butcher a hog. Back home, menfolk might be out huntin' for a spell, then work on splittin' shingles to fix a leak in the roof, plow a field in the spring, or bring in the corn in the fall. It was hard work, but we were never bored.

"But not in a minin' town. In Gallville, things run by the clock. By six o'clock in the morning, every man and boy was out on the road, headin' toward the mine. George carried a pick and auger, a can of blasting powder, fuses, and a tamping rod. He had a small oil lamp on the front of his head, over his cap. They all wore overalls and if they could afford 'em, good boots. We had to buy all this from the company store, so we started out owin' 'em.

"George didn't talk much about what they did in the mine, said he didn't want me to worry about that. But over the winter, I pieced it together from what the other women said— some of the older ones—and from the talk men made on the porch sometimes when outsiders dropped by, tryin' to scare up a union. You'd think all the miners woulda been for it, but after what happened in Mattewan, women begged their men to leave it be. They'd get by, they said. They didn't want their children goin' hungry or cut down by the Pinkerton men. It's amazin' what a body'll put up with to protect their own.

"But they cut our men's wages again. Raised prices at the store. The union men that snuck in from outside started havin' real meetings. They tole us Ohio miners were gettin' seventy-six cents per ton of clean coal to our men's forty-six cents.

Bella

Our men were lucky to bring in two dollars a day. It seemed the owners were just goin' to keep squeezin' until they had every last bit of our blood.

"You'd think they would have seen it coming, but they didn't. You push people hard enough . . . they didn't leave the men no choice."

Chapter Seven

Norah

" Things went along like that for longer than you'd expect possible. Bad as things are, you get used to 'em. Think it's normal. We lived and even had a scrap of happiness now and then.

"Long about February, I had my own bit of sunshine come my way. I didn't have to let out my dress yet, because I couldn't keep even a bite of cornpone down. I was with child. You'da thought I'd been worried, bringin' a child into a town like that, but I think nature has a way of pullin' the gauze over your eyes, makin' the world look softer so your body can focus on growin' the baby, and you can gather strength so you can bear up under what you're gonna face.

Leastwise, that's how it was with me. Suddenly, this little spark o' life held my whole attention. I stopped worryin' 'bout the mine. Things were the way they were and I wasn't gonna change 'em.

"I didn't have no other young-uns to tend to, so I had time to sit and stitch up a few things for the baby. Didn't have no battin' for a baby quilt, but traded some doctorin' for some cattail fluff. Aunt Leila used to line our boots and blankets with that and it worked real well.

"The mine bosses seem to have let up. No mine foremen come by the house tryin' to catch anyone entertainin' a union man. The railroad had plenty of coal cars, so everybody was workin' full weeks and the mine was up and runnin' again after bein' shut down for repairs awhile. There were still the occasional lost fingers, crippled legs, and wrenched backs, but it'd been months since Tessa's man died. Tessa was real nice. Lived three doors down. She helped me learn my way around when we first got there.

"George was a tonnage man now, so he worked fewer hours and had more leeway than the mule skinners and such. Other than a-worryin' 'bout George like I always did when he left me to go down in that black hole, I let myself enjoy the sun peekin' out and the starts I had goin' for a garden, waitin' for the last frost to pass.

"I made up a quilt top and cut a pattern outta the side of a cracker box from the store. Used the rest o' the box to stuff into cracks around the windows to keep the cold out, but it didn't do much good. I woulda needed a hundred cracker boxes. The pattern was kinda like a cat's eye—a large, pointy oval with a smaller one cut out inside. You overlapped it outside point on inside point—real simple, just marked it with some chalk, then moved it around until you had a chain design to follow around. Each woman made her own pattern on the corner squares. Those were just freehanded. I always made a honey bee.

"Anyways, it was long about April when the trouble started. I was over the sickness, the baby was growin' steady inside, but not too big. Didn't have enough food for her to grow big on.

"Some of the men played baseball. It was powerful fun and your granddaddy was a sight to see when he hit that ball and run them bases. Never saw such a pure look o' joy as when he knocked that ball over top of the next house!

"But then things started up again. The owners were back up to their old tricks and the men started thinkin' on a union. We had more than one night meetin' at our place, which put George in considerable danger. Like every man hired back then, he'd signed a *yellow dog* contract, which meant he swore he'd never join a union, let alone start one. The mine owners wanted to keep all the money our men clawed out and dragged up those shafts, not knowin' every minute if the particular tunnel they were in was goin' to come crashin' down on their heads and bury them alive. Almost every man was missin' fingers or had some part of his body that'd been smashed or wrenched so it didn't work right anymore.

"George was the kind of man other men come to. He never spoke two words when one would do, but when he spoke, men listened. George was plum tired when he come home at night, but he never turned anyone away. All he wanted to do was sleep. But after I rustled him up some supper, we'd cover the windows against the lights and the men'd start a coming, one or two at a time. There'd be a quiet knock at the door. Every time I heard it, a soft step on the board, I thought of Mattewan and I struggled to breathe. But we never saw anyone of the mine's hired men. I wondered about that then. Why, in such a small town, the bosses never figured out what was happenin' under their very noses.

"I didn't need to wonder long. They knew, all right. They knew.

"George and some of the other miners been meetin' more regular at our house and a few others and had it all set. They were gonna work a full day the next day, then wait 'til everybody weighed in. Some wanted to go on strike, but George convinced them to try reasonin' with the owners first. He was still afraid of that yellow-dog contract. Still had faith that those no 'counts would do the right thing when faced with plain talk. I think he was so good, he couldn't conceive of any man who didn't have at least one spark of good in him. You just had to reach it. And he didn't want what happened to the folks in Mattewan to happen in Gallville. Their plan was for George and another man to do the talking. They would tell the bosses they wouldn't let the union in if the owners would do right by them. The miners just wanted what they had comin' to 'em.

"All that day, you could feel the excitement in the air. One more day of slavin' for another man's profit. One more day 'til they could hold their heads up and make a fair wage, maybe pay a widow and children a little somethin' when their man got killed. One more day. So that morning, they all went down into the mines like usual.

"But some of those men never come up. 'Round two o'clock the siren went off and we knew. News flew like wildfire down that muddy road. There'd been an explosion in one of the tunnels. The owners blamed it on firedamp, but we all knew it wasn't no accident. Word musta got to them somehow. You can't keep a secret in a town that small. George was in the tunnel that blew, along with some of the main organizers.

"One of the neighbor women sat with me that night. Made me supper, which I couldn't eat. Nothin' left. No man to bury. Had to leave the company house next day. They tacked a notice on my front door. Said I had to clear out by Sunday supper. Less than forty-eight hours from the time they took George's life.

"There was nothin' much to pack, and this time, no mule to carry it anyway. Almost everything we had was from the company store. People came and said their goodbyes. I packed what food I could carry and my fiddle. George's pipe. That's it up on the mantle.

"Tessa stayed up all night with some of the women to finish the baby's quilt, so I had that. But while we was down at the mine gettin' the news, some of the company men snuck back like pole cats and spoilt our weddin' ring quilt. Poured tar on it. They would have smashed my fiddle if they'd seen it, but it was under the bed.

"Come Sunday, I tightened up my boot laces, hoisted up my tote sack, and walked home.

"Wasn't 'til 1933 they 'llowed a union in that mine. Too late to save my George. Or any of the others.

Chapter Eight

1924
ABOARD THE ST. MICHELE
GENOA TO NEW YORK
STEERAGE

Giovanni

"I couldn't believe it! Ten long years, but my internship would soon be over! All of my hard work and staying out of Antonio's way had paid off. I had made no missteps. And now, once I made this violin, and with such a fine piece of wood to work with, I had no doubt I could make an instrument to pass the Master Basso's final test. My father had set aside some money to help me get started. All I had to do was pass this test and I'd be able to set up my own shop.

"But when I did, how would Antonio take it? Had the Master considered how his son would react to my being advanced before him? I knew Antonio. He'd bashed heads for far less, often resulting in his father having to pay his way out of whatever trouble he got himself into.

"But these things must have been far from Master Basso's mind. He told Antonio to close up shop and meet us at home. His tremors grew worse at night. He would start on the new job fresh in the morning.

"Closing up was usually my job. Casting a nervous glance at Antonio, I quietly tucked my piece of wood behind some buckets under the workbench of another apprentice who had worked there in busier times. I'm not sure why, but I didn't want to flaunt it in front of Antonio, or maybe I just didn't want him to know where it was. I would complete my current projects as soon as possible. Then I would retrieve the wood and begin work on my last violin as an apprentice.

"Placing Master Basso's piece of wood on his workbench, I put on my coat and followed him outside and down the darkening street. Antonio never looked up or said a word.

"Then he accepted his father's choice?" Giovanni's companion asked.

"No, I knew he would never let it go, that's why I hid the prize his father had given me, hoping he wouldn't see where I put it. It wasn't until the next day that the depth of Antonio's anger and resentment became apparent."

"That morning, Antonio was not at breakfast. Since he sometimes stayed out all night with his friends, this wasn't completely unusual. His father was not pleased, his mother made excuses for his absence, and I remained silent, looking down at my polenta.

"Finally, the master and I went to the shop, the anticipation of working on the newly commissioned violin lifting his spirits somewhat. His step was light as we made our way around the lake and down the narrow street.

"When we arrived, a few people—fellow shopkeepers and neighbors—were standing outside, looking in the broken window and the open door. They parted to let us in. Most of the completed violins for sale were intact, but the piece of wood we had painstakingly selected yesterday and placed on the master's workbench had been savaged—chopped with an ax into hundreds of splintered pieces.

"I ran to the back of the shop. Running low, I ducked down and there it was, right where I had hurriedly placed it under the former intern's table. Relief flooded through me. I let out a breath and my heart unclenched. My wood was safe. Then I immediately felt guilty.

"Leaving it there, I quickly went back to the front of the shop and began sweeping up the shattered glass and what was left of the master's perfect piece of wood. Master Basso stood at the door, accepted people's murmured condolences and turned away their offers of help. He said we would handle it—not much damage had been done after all. Probably travelers passing through; thieves frightened off before they could steal anything. Yes, he would let them know if they could be of any assistance.

"When the shop had been put to rights, the master sat down heavily on his stool and closed his eyes. The silence hung all around us, pressing on my ears. I did not want him to speak, but I knew he would.

"Giovanni . . . ," he began.

"So much was loaded into that one enunciation of my name: pain, regret, resignation, determination. I slowly walked back, retrieved my piece of wood from behind the bucket, and laid it next to him on the bench. Then I returned to my work. Of course, he would need it now."

"What happened? Did he give another piece of wood? Did Antonio ever come back?"

"Antonio came back. A week, maybe two weeks later. Nothing was ever said. It was as if nothing had happened, but everything had. Master Basso completed Signor Valerio's violin in time for the music festival, and if it wasn't as good as the other piece of wood would have produced, its sound was such that people still asked who made it and Master Basso's reputation was restored.

"But no more mention was made of my making a violin or graduating from my apprenticeship. To his credit, Antonio began applying himself more and managed to put together instruments of almost acceptable value—the best he could do. At the same time, feeling his new power, Antonio began ordering me around when his father wasn't within earshot. Master Basso began taking him on trips when he made them, or to the houses of clients, making introductions, smoothing the way for his future success. I became completely unsure of my place.

"Once Antonio returned, the master barely spoke to me or looked my way, except when he absolutely needed me for tasks Antonio could not do and that he had lost the ability to perform himself.

"Eventually, after working several more years—years well past the normal apprenticeship—I accepted the truth. Master Basso was never going to give me what I needed, my certificate, even though I'd earned it many times over. He could not promote me over his son. Or even with him. There seemed to have been a silent decision made. It was Antonio, first and last, and everyone else be damned.

"Nowhere in Italy could I become an independent luthier without that certificate. No matter how talented, each town required it. How was I ever going to start my life—establish myself, have a family, as my father had done in his profession?"

"I am sorry, my friend. That was not right, what happened to you. You were treated very unfairly—and after years of faithful service," Lorenzo said. "How were you able to leave?

Chapter Nine

1924
ABOARD THE ST. MICHELE
GENOA TO NEW YORK, STEERAGE

Giovanni

"One Sunday, when my father's friend, Mauro, was visiting, he couldn't stop talking about America. He travelled from town to town up and down Italy with his puppets and had recently returned from a long trip to Sicily. Mauro said drought had been bad there that year and many Southern Italians were immigrating to America," said Giovanni.

"Yes, that is why we left," Lorenzo said. "They say land is very good in America and there is plenty of water. My plan is to work for a few years, save enough money to buy a small farm on some good land in a rich valley when the rains return. Over there, under the stairs," Lorenzo pointed, "the men there are miners. The men in the front are skilled with stone. But you are not a miner or a farmer."

"No, but America is a big place. And a new one. Mauro said they don't have strict rules and limits on setting up businesses there. Anyone is free to do whatever work they can. He said I wouldn't need a certificate to make and sell violins. And other than my family, I had no reason to stay. It made sense. Still, I wanted to make sure what Mauro heard about America was true. I asked Mauro many more questions that night and stayed awake thinking of how to do this. I couldn't risk asking too many questions in the city, as it might get back to my master, but I was able to verify Mauro was correct. I could be my own man in America. Soon, I had something of a plan. It wasn't without risk, but I needed to act.

"I am not a thief, but I stayed behind one night and carefully selected a few things—worth much less than my years of uncompensated labor—that I would need and that I could not easily recreate without having access to a complete shop. Two little bottles of varnish, a few small blocks of ebony for the fingerboard, some tools, and some strings. Last, but not least, I chose a thick wedge of wood—Norway maple—the best available in the storage room stacks, and placed all of the items, along with a few coins, in the bottom of the case my father provided for my journey. After many tears, I left my family home that night, knowing I would probably never see them again. Branded as a thief from that day on, I could never return to Italy."

Both men were silent for a moment.

"So, there you have my story. When we get to New York, I will make the best violin I can, and with the money I make from selling it, I will open my own shop in New York. I will make the world's most beautiful violins!"

"Then here is to your success!" Lorenzo raised his glass, "*Salut!*"

Bella

Through the rest of the voyage to America, Giovanni got to know many of his other shipmates. Some, like his bunkmate, were fellow Italians. A few had daughters of marriageable age, but none interested him. His ticket did not include a private berth, so his bunk became both his sleeping and living quarters for the trip. To forestall homesickness, he placed a picture of his mother on the inside lid of his small trunk, so he would see it every morning and every evening. He did not suffer from seasickness, but many did, particularly the children. As washing facilities were limited, he learned to live with the ever-present sour smells emanating from the bodies and bedclothes of his fellow passengers. His father had given him enough money to travel in second class—a definite improvement from steerage, offering an extra meal and access to much fresher air—but he chose to focus on his goals and save his money.

Having no idea what to expect, he was still overwhelmed when he caught his first glimpse of the Statue of Liberty. First and second class passengers disembarked at the Hudson and East River piers, passing through customs with hardly a hiccup. Giovanni and the rest of the immigrants were taken to Ellis Island, where they endured long waits for medical and legal inspections before being allowed to enter New York. The legal inspections consisted of little more than checking their names against the ship's manifest, but they were a lot more thorough with the medical exams.

Tuberculosis and other diseases were of great concern, and Giovanni watched sadly as some of his new friends were sent to another room to wait. Unbeknownst to them, doctors observed each person from above as they came in and waited in line, watching for any sign of weakness. Labored breathing might be indicative of heart problems and any strange behaviors might be signs of mental illness. As they passed, if a doctor felt that person needed to be examined more completely, they would indicate the probable condition in chalk on their clothing. An X within a circle meant that person had a definite disease, the letter B indicated back problems, and Ct meant eye disease.

An eye disease called trachoma, which caused blindness and often lead to death was of great concern, as was tuberculosis, as there was no known cure for either of them at the time.

Those not passing their exams were sent to a room, from which they would be sent back to Europe on the next ship. Sick children age twelve and up were included in this number and sent back to their home harbor solo. Sick children under the age of twelve were also sent back, but one of the parents had to go back with them. It was heart wrenching to watch the difficult decisions and tearful separations.

Most made it through, but the waiting was hell. After all that way . . . to be turned back was every immigrant's worst fear.

Giovanni, being young and healthy, made it through in only half a day, including standing in line to exchange his few Italian coins into American money. The sun was low in the sky already, but landing card in hand, he gripped his case, pulled his hat down against the sun, and walked toward the ferry and his new future.

NEW YORK
1928

Giovanni couldn't believe it had been almost two years already since he stepped off the ferry. Lorenzo had insisted he come stay with them and since he knew no one else in New York, Giovanni had accepted, as long as his new friend would accept at least a little something in the way of rent to share a room with Lorenzo's two sons and a bit more toward meals. The arrangement suited them both. Giovanni enjoyed the noisy, comfortable family life. It made him even more determined to establish a home here so he could someday have a family of his own. He planned on staying with Lorenzo's family until he got his bearings.

Things were different here. Although Mantua was a city, it was separated from this American city not only by thousands of physical miles across an ocean, but thousands more in cultural miles. Everything moved faster here. And the noise! Each neighborhood was a different nation it seemed. All jostling shoulder to shoulder, trying to get a firm grip on this new land, their new home, America!

Walking down any street he heard Italian, German, Polish, Yiddish, Gaelic . . . and everywhere, heavily accented English. It was overwhelming, but it also fed Giovanni's sense of adventure. He found work in a music shop repairing violins and other stringed instruments. They also sold instruments, so Giovanni, on his own time, used the basement of his new friends' home to construct a violin. When it was finished, he brought it to the owner, who agreed to place it for sale on consignment—taking a hefty percentage for himself, of course.

Of a much higher quality than the other instruments in the man's shop, Giovanni's violin sold within days of being showcased in the window. Since the majority of the neighborhood was Polish, Giovanni couldn't understand any of the lengthy negotiations between the owner and the man buying his violin. He surreptitiously watched as the customer paid, but as he wasn't totally familiar with American denominations yet, he couldn't tell what his instrument finally sold for. From the greedy look on his boss's face, it was a lot. And what he paid Giovanni was definitely less. He was pretty sure he wasn't getting the full amount owed him, but he had no recourse but to accept what he was given.

Realizing how lucrative this deal had been, the shop owner eagerly wanted Giovanni to make him another violin, but Giovanni put him off. He had enough ebony, string, and varnish to make one or two more, but would have to purchase another block of wood for the body—he'd only had room in his case for one piece. No, buying the wood would take all his profits and he didn't even know if he could find wood of the quality he needed here. It's not like there were a lot of trees in New York, and even if there were, it would take years for the wood to age properly.

Lorenzo's home was often filled with people. Relatives and other recently arrived Italian immigrants were welcomed by his generous and long-suffering wife, Teresa, to stay for a few days or just share a meal on their way to the train station. Dinners were long, loud, and delicious. One of Lorenzo and Teresa's guests was heading to a coalmining town in West Virginia, traveling part of the way with another family aiming farther—all the way to California. It was said the climate there was warm and perfect for growing olives, like Italy. Giovanni wasn't interested in mining or farming, but a city perched on the blue Pacific sounded perfect for him—San Francisco. Urban enough to have a market for his violins, but he hoped not as greedy and grasping as New York, or as miserable in the winter.

Having made up his mind, he packed his few belongings back into his small trunk and went with his new friends to the train station the next morning. The young father bragged that the coal mining company who'd hired him, via the labor agent who had recruited him in New York, was paying full fares for his ticket, his wife, and their children. What he didn't know, is that they would be charged for those tickets on the other end, and 'allowed' to work them off, which many never could, resulting in a form of indentured servitude. Giovanni was able to pay for his ticket himself, using about half of the money he had left. Thirty-two dollars. He chose not to pay the extra ten dollars for a Pullman bed. He wanted to save every penny. Who knew how much things would cost in San Francisco?

Chapter Ten

1966
RED SLEEVE WV

Norah

" Aunt Leila helped me with the birthing.

"The baby come hard, like she didn't want to be born—leastwise not in no mountain cabin. But she was strong and healthy. I named her Elsie May. She was a beauty from the day she was born and knew it. All she had to do was flash those green eyes and toss that mess o' red curls and menfolk'd come a runnin'!

"She had Grandpa wrapped around her little finger from the day she was born. Aunt Leila had her number, though. She put that child in her place more than once. She tole me once that Elsie was like a strong river. Too strong to dam up, so our job was to direct her course, not stop her from runnin', even if it was away from us. It was good advice. Wouldn't a done no good if I'd tried to hold her here. Once she had her mind set, that girl couldn't been stopped with a double load of dynamite!

"Time passed.

"Comin' back to the holler, well, I knew then how lucky I was. It was like I never left. I made my way helpin' Aunt Leila with her doctorin' and took care of Grandpa more and more as he got on in years. He was kinda like I am now—everything works, but just takes a little longer to get goin' in the morning!"

Will laughed.

"You laugh now, Will, but your time's comin'! I do look pretty funny hobbling around here in the morning like an ole three-legged dog.

"Big things happened in the outside world that year, but we didn't know much about it until later. World War I had come and gone and World War II hadn't started yet. But things wasn't easy. After the big crash in '29, jobs dried up and folks who'd left for the city come back to the mountains. Too many people and not enough land to scratch out a living. Then there was the drought. The land just plain tuckered out.

"I think that's when your ma turned on livin' here. We usually had enough to eat, but no money to buy things. And the more she grew, the more she wanted. At nine or ten, she started wantin' pretty ribbons. By the time she was eleven or twelve, well . . . she wanted the moon, that girl.

"But, in '29, before things got hard, Elsie was only seven years old and still happy as punch with a piece of hard candy from Grandpa's pocket or findin' a bird's nest in a tree. And of course, any story from Giovanni, a newcomer to the holler about that time."

Chapter Eleven

1966
RED SLEEVE, WV

Norah

"Late that summer, 'bout this time o' year, some Italians come through here from New York. A young family, real nice, passed on through to Gallville, where the man had a job waitin' for him in the mine. He was one of the lucky ones. Times were startin' to git hard and he was lucky to get the job. I heard rumors they were tryin' to get a union out there again, but didn't hold out much hope. I just hoped things'd be better for them than when George and I were there.

"Another man, a young man named Giovanni, not a miner, decided to stop off here. No one knew why, but since the trains ran more and more people out to the mines or further west, we just accepted newcomers, as long as they didn't cause any trouble. Most didn't stay long.

"We heard the MacIntosh's took him in—let him sleep in their barn in exchange for helpin' out. It was obvious right off he weren't no farmer, but any man can learn to chop wood and carry water, and Martha told Aunt Leila the young Italian seemed willing. He worked for his keep and didn't carouse, so they kept him on. We didn't hear much more about him 'til spring.

"First I ever saw of Giovanni was the top of his head. When Grandpa and I came across a hill from our place, where it sloped down into the MacIntosh's meadow, he was bendin' down to brush some dust off his shoe. I saw a full head of thick, black curls shinin' in the sun. It was a warm afternoon, but the nights were still cold, so he wore wool pants and a coat—worn and of a foreign cut, but nice. He looked up to see who was coming. His eyes was big, dark liquid brown, like a deer's, set deep into smooth, olive skin. No freckles like me. He smiled, shy like.

"A minute later, Grandpa and I come out the trees at the bottom of the path and headed toward the barn. They were havin' a dance and both Grandpa and I was playin'. MacIntosh had the banjo and o' course, Uncle Levi always brought moonshine for the men—and some of the women, truth be told! Since Giovanni slept in the barn, he'd given up his peace for that night, anyway.

"Most the holler came. Lookin' back, I think they had those dances to keep the young men from fightin' after bein' cooped up all winter—helped 'em blow off steam and let 'em keep their teeth.

"Oh, I love to hear you laugh! It's been a while since a young person's laugh filled this house. I'm so glad you found me and took the time to come all this way, Will.

"Anyway, later that night Grandpa, MacIntosh, and I was playin' up a storm. We'd been at it a couple hours and was 'bout ready to rest a spell. It was cold outside, but sweat was rollin' down my back we'd been playin' so hard. Aunt Leila kept an eye on Elsie for me, makin' sure she didn't wander outside where the men and shine was. All the children played together on the floor, in and out of everyone's feet. People danced and the old folks sat and tapped their feet. After the men had gone outside to get their courage up, they threw down a piece of wood floor and they'd take to cloggin'—you know cloggin'? They'd see who could do better than the next one, tryin' to impress the women. Just as we were buildin' up to a grand finale, Grandpa broke a string. Grandpa didn't usually swear, but a few choice words came out then. Strings were hard to come by and he didn't have any extra.

"Giovanni'd been standin' on the side, just listening, not dancing. When he saw Grandpa'd lost a fiddle string, he went up to him and started sayin' something. None of us could understand, so he made signs with his hands for Grandpa to wait. He hurried to the dark back of the barn and we could hear him goin' up the ladder to the hay loft, rummagin' around. He come back out with something in his hands. With a look that asked permission, he took Grandpa's fiddle and replaced that broken string quicker than anything. Where he got it was a mystery. I watched his fine, long fingers—he obviously knew his way around a violin. He wanted to replace all of 'em, but Grandpa wouldn't let him. He didn't like owin' anyone.

"Grandpa invited him up to our place the next day so's we could make him a good meal as a thank you. He seemed to understand well enough and accepted. They must been starvin' him at MacIntosh's, 'cause he ate every bite that night and took seconds when they were offered. He came to visit often after that. He'd bring Elsie a carved bird or me some flowers. He even made Aunt Leila a new pipe once. He more than paid for the beans, greens, and cornbread he put away.

"I was often away that spring and summer, gatherin' herbs or goin' with Aunt Leila to a birthing. There was a brand new schoolhouse now, and I made sure Elsie went while she could. Nothin' is for certain in the mountains. Sometimes there was school, sometimes not, back then. School teachers didn't last long if they was from outside and even local marms had to quit when they got married and started families, so school was kinda hit and miss. I wanted Elsie to get at least her letters and cipherin' down good before this one left, so she could hold her own in life.

"Early mornin' while the dew's still on's a good time to collect most herbs. It keeps in the power so the sun don't take it. And you don't wash 'em or you lose the oils. Anyway, so I'd usually be out when Elsie left to walk to school.

"Grandpa Harley and Giovanni took t'each other right away and most afternoons, after his chores were done, Giovanni'd walk over to our place and I'd find them visitin' on the porch, Elsie at his feet. Grandpa didn't learn no Italian, but Giovanni was a quick study and he could soon say a few words in English—enough to make himself understood. Elsie liked to play teacher, helpin' him read her primer.

"After supper, he'd just sit and listen to Grandpa play. When Grandpa's rheumatism got bad so's he couldn't hold the bow long, I'd take a turn. My fiddle didn't sound as good as Grandpa's, but I played my best. Giovanni sometimes got a thoughtful look on his face.

"After a while, he got comfortable with us, and I guess feelin' a need to contribute, one night, Giovanni pulled out a small, square leather bound book he had and read from it to us by the kerosene lantern light or the fire if we were inside. Poems, mostly. We didn't understand his words, but I closed my eyes, I swear, his voice sounded like a stream burblin' and singin' across the rocks. I never hear'd Italian again, but the way he spoke it, it was soft. I only learnt a few words of it. And you could hear somethin' else running deep under those words—a powerful need. Every man has to find his way—has to have a purpose. Giovanni wasn't a farmer, what was his purpose I wondered?

"What was Giovanni de Mantua doin' in these mountains?"

Chapter Twelve

1966
RED SLEEVE WV

Norah

"You have to remember, it'd been eight years since George died. We were only married little over a year and what with him workin' the long hours at the mine . . . we barely knew each other. He was my husband and I was his wife, but if he thought of anything besides workin' and eating, I didn't know it. I was too young to ask. Back then men spent time with menfolk, and women with womenfolk mostly. Things is different today. I wonder sometimes now if he was lonely, if he ever had thoughts or dreams he couldn't share. I hope not. I wouldn't like to think that. I hope he was happy. He seemed so.

"Here, now . . . don't listen to an old woman ramble on. Let me get you some supper. I'll tell you more after we eat."

"George was a good man—good and brave. I hope I was a good wife to him, but things were different when I met

Giovanni. I'd grow'd up a heap. I was no longer a young girl. I had my place here. At twenty-seven, a widow and a mother, I put food on the table and with the help of my family, I didn't need a man. And Grandpa seemed to have given up on findin' me one when it was clear I didn't want another husband.

"Giovanni was different—and not just because he was foreign. I enjoyed looking on his hands as he held his book and how patient he was when Elsie'd ask him to tell her 'nother story about life back in Italy. He told her fantastical things. Like he said they had stores there that only sold one thing! Like one for bread and one just for cheese. Another one for all kinds of meat. And music everywhere. Italians loved music, Giovanni told us.

"I don't know if he made that part up about the stores—I've never been to Italy to see for myself—but it kept Elsie entertained hearin' about it. She told him when she grew up she was goin' to see Rome, Milan, and Paris—all those places he talked about. She'd make up little plays and have us all act out the parts. When she finally fell asleep in front of the fire and Grandpa'd shuffled off to bed, Giovanni'd tuck his book back into his coat, take out his fine handkerchief—it was always clean—wipe his face and settle into Grandma Louise's rocker, and wait for me to rosin up my bow.

"That's when I'd play. Music is powerful good. I'd play all the pain I left back in Gallville. The men buried under tons of dirt and rock. Tessa's face when they told her her man wasn't comin' home. The bill from the company store that just kept getting' bigger and we could never pay. The sight of that lean-to they called a house, the roof leakin' every time the sky so much as spit. With a good rain, we might as well a' lived outside. I remembered a sick boy shiverin' from the fever I come to tend with the few dried herbs I had left, his sister layin' close beside him, givin' up her own half of a thin blanket, tryin' to keep her feverish brother alive through the night. And the final, rippin' pain that tore through me when I heard that siren and knew my George was gone. The only thing kept me goin' was that spark of life inside me. I know'd I had to make a life for my child.

"We didn't have a common language, but I wanted Giovanni to feel who we were, who I was.

"Then, when words failed me, I left that place in my mind and played the beauty of the mountains, the speckled light on the creek with fine, clean water runnin' fast along its course. Because that's in our blood, too. The good corn in the field. The sweet smell of the wood fire. Aunt Leila's pipe. The feelin' of solid when the winter wind whipped around the cabin and we were warm inside with food enough to last 'til spring. Elsie's red curls bouncin' and shinin' in the sun, her eyes sparkling when Giovanni talked about what the women wore in Milan, or their two heads—one full of red curls, one of black— puzzlin' together over Elsie's primer with the warm smell of cornbread in the oven and stew bubblin' on the stove.

"Giovanni sat still, his eyes closed, barely rocking, an inward expression on his face. I expect he had his own pain to remember and I hope my playin' soothed it some.

"There's powerful good in music. Don't you forget it, child.

"Nothing that good can stay, of course. It just seems to be the way of things, but something bad has to enter. By the door or the window or pushin' in through the cracks, hurt finds a way in. And so it was for us.

"Fetch me my fiddle, now. I've a mind to play."

Chapter Thirteen

1966
RED SLEEVE, WV

Norah

"You sleep all right last night? That tickin' needs to be changed out. I know it's not what you're used to. Still can't believe you found me and come all the way from New York to visit. But I'm shore glad you did. Thought I'd never learn what happened to your ma. Hadn't heard a word from her after she left. Glad she found what she was a lookin' for. We all have to follow our own star.

"You said you wanted to learn 'bout life in the holler, so I asked Karl to stop by on his way down to Langley's place. He's buildin' hisself a log cabin with some of the menfolk. The old one burned down. He says you can watch or help, your choice. But if'n you're gonna work, you should change those shoes. I think some of Grandpa's old boots'll fit you. You look to be about the same size. And dig in that trunk for some gloves. I think there's a pair in there. I don't use 'em. My fingers is used to rough.

"You'll probably only last the mornin', so I'll have somethin' for you to eat for dinner. It'll be ready when the sun is high, but it'll keep on the stove, so come back anytime. If you work that long, they'll feed you."

LATER THAT DAY

"Thanks, Karl! How's the cabin comin'? . . . Good, good, pleased he could be of some help to you. He's a city boy, but has a willin' heart. Tell Martha thank you for the pickles. I do love her pickles!"

"Well, grandson, it looks like you made it the morning and then some. Proud of you, but you look plum tuckered out. Pull out a chair out here on the porch. There's a breeze and shade on this side. Bring your plate out here. No, I had my dinner. Supper's on the stove—be ready come dark. I'll get back to the tellin' as soon as you're situated."

THAT NIGHT

"I've been settin' here, thinkin' 'bout the mountain. The way it was then. But I was rememberin' before that spring. 1929 was a long, cruel winter. That fall, we heard tell about somethin' bad happened in the city, but it didn't affect us for a while. Wasn't 'til later it had a name. The Great Depression. And that stayed with us quite a while.

"But we didn't know how bad it was gonna get, so we just carried on like usual. I showed Giovanni where the spring greens and such grew. Made him a dandelion salad. Tender, wild onions. You can et the young greens offa lotta plants if you're careful—we'd have salt pork and greens most ever' day.

We'd have to wait 'til fall for the mushrooms. They be comin' on now. If'n you want, I'll take you out tomorrow and show you some.

"Lots of berries in the holler, but not all the berries come at the same time. They come in waves, with strawberries comin' first, then elderberries, then huckleberries—my favorite—and blackberries. I secretly hoped Giovanni would stay with us long enough to enjoy my huckleberry pie.

"We had a new teacher that spring, so Elsie was happy. She loved school and still got to come home and visit with Giovanni when he came over most nights. They kept at his learnin' English, too.

"Aunt Leila'd passed that winter. She'd been slowin' down, but didn't want no doctor. Wasn't really sick, she said, just tired. Said livin' ninety-seven years on this earth was all anyone could ask for. Didn't want to leave her home. I moved over there for a while. She seemed to enjoy the company and I asked her every question I could think of about medicines. There was so much I felt I didn't know and not enough time left for Aunt Leila to teach me. Weren't no one else to teach me but her.

"She kept more and more to her bed, until one day she didn't rise. Laid her to rest up the mountain like she wanted, once the ground thawed. I go up there sometimes, just to be near her. Or I used to, when I could make the climb. Good woman. Aunt Leila never said an ill word about anyone.

"She loved sassafras tea. I forgot to tell you when you come in, but I made you some in a jar in the window, there. I can't remember a thing anymore. You'll wonder what kind of grandma I am, lettin' you sit there on the porch on a hot day without fetchin' you so much as a glass of tea to quench your thirst! And some huckleberry pie. Yes, I made that for you, too.

"I love pie better 'n a cat loves sweet milk. I really do.

"Right, back to my story.

"Giovanni. Well, he had a cough started that winter. Lotta folks get coughs that time o' year. I made him up some red horsemint tea. When that didn't fix him up, I boiled up some wild cherry bark, black gum bark, and whole rat's vein—put in a whole pint of sugar. That syrup helped some, but his cough didn't go away.

"When blood started spottin' his handkerchief, I knew his cough was more than any medicine could cure. He had the consumption, what you call tuberculosis now. It wasn't a matter of *if* he was going to die, but when. People sometimes lived years with it, but his was bad. No way of knowin' how much time he had, but I'd keep him going as long as I could.

"We never spoke of it. I made him poultices and teas to ease the coughing. He'd have good weeks and then a bad spell. A long-term sickness don't travel an even path. It meanders up, down, and around the mountain as it draws you along. When Aunt Leila knew she was at the end of her own road, knowin' it was her time to go, she gave Giovanni her cabin. It was smaller than ours, one room and a narrow, back area Grandpa made her for dryin' and storin' up her plants, but it was solid and saw him through that winter. Much warmer than the MacIntosh's barn.

"First thing Giovanni did when he moved in was clear out that back room and help me carry Aunt Leila 's jars and dried herbs and doctorin' equipment and such to my place. Then he started workin' on something in there. He was all secret about it. Wouldn't let anyone see it.

"Henry brung up more firewood for the winter, like he did every year for Aunt Leila, but there was quite a bit already out in back, so Giovanni had plenty. Henry shoulda put the older, dryer wood up to the front to use first and stacked the newer, wetter wood in back, but he was always in a hurry and didn't do it right even when Leila was alive. Other than Henry, no one saw much of Giovanni 'cept when he come over to hear Grandpa and me play of an evening, or he let me doctor him when his cough was bad.

"It wasn't until spring solstice we finally seen what he'd been up to all winter, Elsie and me."

Chapter Fourteen

WINTER 1929
RED SLEEVE, WV

Giovanni

The cabin was snug. Giovanni'd brought in enough wood for the night, stoked the fire, and now sat, warm and dry, at the table in Norah's aunt's small, but comfortable cabin. He would miss the woman. She was a skilled healer, just as capable as the doctors in Mantua even though as far as he knew, she had no formal training. These people had been so good to him.

Gripped by a sudden fit of coughing, he pulled out his handkerchief, covered his mouth, and bent over at the waist. When the coughing subsided, pushing on his legs, he slowly sat back up, struggling to pull in a full lungful of air.

He looked down at his hands and opened up the handkerchief. Another dark blotch bloomed across the soft, white cloth. He had known for a while this was more than a winter cough. Consumption. He'd seen several people suffering from it on the ship, turned sadly away at Ellis Island. He'd tried to avoid them onboard, without being unkind, but he must have contracted it anyway, or from any number of people jammed into New York City over the past two years. It was a very contagious disease. Only Norah's teas and poultices provided any relief, but he knew there was no cure.

Just when he thought . . . after everything he went through to rebuild his dream . . . and then finding someone like Norah . . . and a place as beautiful as these mountains . . . to have it all taken away . . . to lose everything all over again after leaving his home, surviving an unscrupulous boss and harsh life in New York, making it this far . . . and now he had something—someone—to live for . . . someone he wanted to take care of . . . and he had nothing to give her! She was taking care of him, and there was nothing he could do about it.

Alone in the darkening cabin, Giovanni gave himself over to grief and misery.

When his breathing calmed, he wadded up his handkerchief and mopped his eyes.

Okay. Enough self-pity. He didn't have time to waste. He may not be able to marry Norah and take her to San Francisco to share a new life with him, but there was something he could give to her. Something he hoped she'd treasure long after he was gone.

He lifted one of the kerosene lanterns off the table in the main room and placed it on a shelf above the workbench in the back where Norah's Aunt had dried and stored her herbs. He didn't know how long he had, so he'd better get started now.

Bringing his case over to the bench, working quickly, but carefully, he removed and hung his steel tools, the jar of varnish, and remaining sets of strings. Arranging the patterns and forms within reach, satisfied he had done all he could for tonight, he stoked the fire again and after another coughing spell, got into bed under a layer of thick covers.

Watching the firelight cast dancing shadows on the cabin walls, as always, his thoughts turned to Norah. Picturing her long, lithe body—strong and confident—her calf muscles bunching with every step as she easily climbed up the mountain paths in front of him in search of mushrooms or herbs, occasionally waiting for him to catch up, her hair glinting copper as she moved in and out of the shadows of rocks and trees. She was a beautiful woman, but also a talented one.

He could not ask Norah to marry him—she'd already lost one husband and he had nothing to offer her—but he could make her a violin worthy of her skill. In another world, she could have become a famous violinist. Her playing was so pure and passionate. He wanted to tell her how she made him feel when she sat on the porch at sunset, closed her eyes and lost herself in her music, or kissed her daughter's forehead when she tucked a quilt around her. But he couldn't. Even if his English had been good enough, he didn't know if he could express what he felt. That whenever he was near her, it was all he could do not to stare into her green eyes or reach out and touch her glowing skin or gather her long hair against his face and breathe in her scent.

He didn't know where or how, but tomorrow, he would find some wood. It's not like he needed to save his money to continue on to California. Even if he wanted to, which he didn't now that he'd found Norah, he knew the chances of his surviving the trip west were not good. And now, the thought of being anywhere in the world without Norah tasted dry and empty.

The mountains were blanketed in spruce and maple, but he couldn't just chop down a tree then wait five or ten years for it to season. He didn't have five or ten years. Even if he did, he'd have to chop down quite a few trees to find one with wood suitable in tone and grain for making a fine instrument.

MacIntosh's brother, Earl, the local blacksmith, made some furniture on the side. Maybe he would have something or know where he could find it. He'd go see him tomorrow.

EARL'S SHOP

"Well, I've got some red spruce here," Earl said, "only been cut about three years, though. Probably not what you're looking for, right?"

"No, something older . . . ," he looked around the man's workshop, ". . . and stripes like that . . . ," Giovanni said, pointing to a dramatically patterned dining table top in progress.

"Yes, that's a beautiful piece," Earl agreed. "Maple. What size you lookin' for?"

"No too large," Giovanni said. With his hands he indicated a piece a couple of inches by a couple of feet and ten inches wide. "Can be small, but needs thick," he added, pantomiming splitting the wood down the middle lengthwise. "Put together," he said butting the sides of his two hands up against each other, showing how he would glue the two pieces together.

"That I don't have, friend," Earl said, "large or small, but I'll keep on the lookout. If you wait 'til spring, the O'Reilly's'll be tearing down their old barn that half burned down last fall. Might be something you could use in there."

Giovanni smiled sadly, "*Grazie mille* . . . thank you," he said and turned to walk home.

The temperature dropped quickly in the mountains, so when he got back, before he entered the cabin, he stopped at the lean-to and brought in some more firewood. Aunt Leila'd put in plenty for the winter. In front were several rows of cord wood Henry had brought over, and what looked like older wood behind.

Grabbing some canvas work gloves from the cabin, pulling them on as he ran back, Giovanni turned up the collar of his coat and worked steadily to remove and restock the newer cordwood to the right of the lean-to shielding it from snow and rain. In less than an hour, he'd worked his way to the back of the stack.

Pitch dark now, he knew he should wait until morning, but he couldn't. Hanging the lantern on a hook in front of and above the rows of old firewood, he began a methodical search, not wanting to miss it if it existed. The load of wood Henry brought was red spruce. The wood in this section was mainly spruce, too, but with some sugar maple mixed in, grayed and split on the ends, the bark falling off. Several pieces were large enough, but on closer inspection, only a few had the tiger striping he was looking for.

Trying to tamp down his excitement, Giovanni narrowed the selection down to two thick pieces of sugar maple along with some spruce for the top. Lifting them up, cradling them in his arms, he carried them inside, placing them on the table as if they were made of precious gold. Then he went back for one more piece: a short, squat log that looked promising.

The whole piece turned out to be the one. Once he quarter-cut into it the next morning, like a wedding cake, the wedge he removed was perfect. Knocking on it with the first knuckle of his left hand, the excellent tone it produced made him smile. And the tiger stripes fanned out from close together to flaring farther apart, matching perfectly when he cut the wedge lengthwise and placed the two pieces side by side. Sugar maple would be a challenge to work with—it was an extremely hard wood—but it should last a very long time.

This piece of wood sounded even better than the one he selected for Master Basso years ago, and Norah was certainly a more deserving recipient.

He couldn't wait to get started!

Chapter Fifteen

1966
RED SLEEVE, WV

Norah

" That winter was harsh, but we got us an early spring. It was a week before my birthday."

"How old were you then?" Will asked.

"It was 1930, so I musta turned twenty-five that year. I plum forgot 'cause since Aunt Leila passed, ain't nobody to remind me. Elsie was still a child and didn't think on things like that yet, and Grandpa could barely remember his own name, let alone his birthday.

"I wish you could have seen it! The mountain, I mean. The mountain just busts out with life in spring. Lady slippers, ferns unfurlin', reachin' for the sun, and frogs waking up from the mud. Deep, purrin' croaks of the males tryin' to get the attention of the female frogs all swole up with spawn. Even the dogwood dressed for church. Azaleas so pink they'd hurt your eyes. It's late in the summer now, comin' on fall. Maybe you can come back sometime in the spring and see it for yourself. I'd like that.

"But back to my story . . . Giovanni just come out of a bad spell and with the sun on his face, looked almost as healthy and strong as when he'd arrived in our holler. It had only been two years, but I couldn't remember what lonely felt like. It was as if he'd been in our lives forever. I knew by then how I felt.

"He must have finished whatever he'd been workin' on, because he took most his suppers regular with us again.

"One late afternoon he was settin' on the porch when I got home. I'd been to the Cooper's place to help Martha's second to youngest ease her pain some, get the swellin' near her shoulder down. Their ornery mule swift kicked at that girl's head and if she hadn't ducked, woulda kilt her. As it was he broke her collarbone. Most mules is docile, but that'n wasn't.

"Anyway, by the time I got home, it was gettin' dark and I was tired and hungry. I saw Giovanni sittin' on the porch steps awaitin' on me with a grin as wide as the creek at Beaver's Dam. I didn't know what he was grinnin' for, it'd take me at least another hour to fix supper and it was dark already.

"But he and Elsie'd taken care of that and fixed me supper that night. Giovanni'd stoked the wood stove fire up and Elsie did the rest. She made pretty good hambone beans and some cornbread. We was runnin' low on honey, but still had enough 'til we could steal some from the bees in a few weeks, when it warmed up some more.

"I could feel the excitement rollin' off Giovanni in sheets, but waited for him to share whatever news he had. Maybe he had family arrivin' from Italy or some other news from his home. I hoped his news wasn't goin' to take him away from us. I knew he couldn't stay forever, but I was hoping to spend whatever time he had left with the man I now know'd I loved.

Whatever the news was, Grandpa seemed in on it, too. He had a glint in his eye and ate his supper faster than usual. He was havin' a good night and recognized ever'body.

Bella

"Finally, when we'd done the washin' up and gathered 'round the fire after supper, Grandpa and I got out our fiddles to play, but Grandpa took mine from my hands and gave Giovanni a nod. Giovanni tried to drag it out, but finally reached back to his coat, which was layin' on the wood box by the door, and from under its folds, pulled out the most beautiful instrument I'd ever seen.

"His eyes shone as he placed it gently in my hands. He looked pleased as punch. I swallowed hard. It was so much better'n my Sears & Roebuck fiddle I couldn't believe he meant for it to be mine. Where he got such an instrument, I couldn't imagine. I was afraid Grandpa's feelings would be hurt because he and Aunt Leila worked so hard to buy my catalogue fiddle for me, but I should have known Grandpa held no grudge. He looked as excited as Giovanni! Besides, Grandpa wanted Elsie to learn to play and this way she'd have her own violin should she ever decide to take it up.

"That guilt relieved, I allowed myself to tremble with the thrill of holdin' such a fine fiddle. In a trance, I lifted it up, tucked it under my chin, bow poised over the first string, afraid to play lest it not sound as beautiful as it looked. I didn't need to worry, for from the first note I realized what a treasure I now possessed. It sounded like honey and sunshine, the singin' creek, thunderstorms, and Elsie laughing.

"Elsie could not contain herself. She must have been in on the secret, because she 'bout burst to tell me."

"And he made it himself! Giovanni made that violin for you, Mama! That's what he's been workin' on all winter! Isn't it beautiful?"

"Giovanni leaned forward, carefully wrappin' his mouth around each word, anxious for me to understand his English, 'Bella . . . like you . . . your music . . . *Bellisima!* Beautiful. Her name is Bella.'"

Chapter Sixteen

Norah

" It was a fine summer. The rest of that year was like livin' in a story. We just floated through on happiness. Early summer, after the garden was in and school was out, I often took Elsie down to the creek for picnics. We made Scotch eggs . . . your mama ever make those for you? Guess not, well, first you boil up some eggs, peel 'em, then grind up some sausage meat, flavor it with sage and such and then press it all around each egg. They look kinda like meat baseballs at that point. Then you dip 'em in some beaten raw egg and roll 'em around in a bowl of dried breadcrumbs. Then you put 'em in a Dutch oven, like that one there, pile some coals on top and let them bake 'til the meat's done. They make great travelin' food—breakfast all in a bite, or you can slice 'em up pretty and et 'em that way.

"Giovanni contributed to our meals, too. The family he

traveled with from New York had given him a big block of this hard, kinda light yeller cheese and a string of dried garlic before they left. He took some of the same cornmeal we made cornbread out of, put it in a pot with some water, covered it and cooked it down for a long time with some o' the garlic. Then he grated up some of that cheese and stirred it in with a hunk of butter. You could eat it lots of ways, but if we left the cheese out, Grandpa liked it just plain with milk and sugar, for breakfast. He called it polenta. Said his mama used to make it a lot, but it was just cornmeal made fancy.

"The teacher in town asked if she could give Elsie some advanced English and Math lessons a few afternoons a week. Elsie was such an eager learner she said. She thought she would make a fine teacher herself some day. I tried not to mind, but I did a little. The teacher could offer her things I couldn't. I said yes, because I knew Elsie needed to grow.

"On those afternoons, with Elsie away, after gittin' Grandpa settled on the porch or in his bed for a nap, I took to walking up Willow Creek as far as I could, stoppin' off to visit Aunt Leila's final restin' place. It was peaceful there. Felt like church, only better.

"I'd just set there in the still, breathing in the quiet, watching the clear water ripple over my bare feet when I sat to cool off before goin' back to make supper. Giovanni started comin' with me. If it was a really warm day, we'd stretch out under the willow tree that hanged over the water, layin' back on the soft moss, lookin' up through the bright, yellow-green, veined leaves into the sky. Giovanni's English was gettin' better, but mostly we didn't talk at all.

"Later that Fall, when none of my medicines helped him much anymore, he took to his bed. Elsie'd grown very attached to Giovanni and was angry with me that I couldn't fix things. She wanted me to take him to a 'real' doctor and wouldn't listen when I told her that even if I had the money, it wouldn't do no good. No one could save him. She never did forgive me for that.

"That last few days I stayed with him there. He wrote a letter to his mother I promised to send for him. He wanted to be buried up on Willow Creek, but didn't feel he had the right, since he wasn't family. But by then we all felt he was family and I told him Aunt Leila'd have words with me if I buried him anywheres else. I could tell it made him happy, and gave him some measure o' peace, so that's what we did.

"Well, that's near most the story. I know you need to leave soon, that school out in California gave you a scholarship, you'd best make sure you get there on time. Henry can give you a ride to the train station day after tomorrow. I'm gittin' tired. I'm goin' to go in and lay down a spell."

"Okay, but tomorrow I want to hear it all," Will said, "or at least as much as you are willing to tell me. Mother and I had a major falling out over this. She never talked about you, or this place. I only found out she was from Appalachia when I needed my birth certificate for my passport application. We were going to Europe for graduation.

"She said she was going to send all the paperwork in for me, but I wanted to be responsible and save her some time— she was always so busy with fundraisers and her work at the symphony. I found hers along with father's and my birth certificates in the back of the family Bible.

"Mine was on top. William David Carmichael III—my name's so long it hardly fit in the box. That's when she came in and grabbed the Bible and the rest of the birth certificates out of my hand, but not before I saw *Red Sleeve, West Virginia* on hers.

"Mother—Eleanor—no one ever called her Elsie in New York—had an absolute fit when I told her I found out she was from West Virginia, not New York as we always thought. When I discovered I had a grandmother still alive and was coming to see you, she threatened to leave me out of her will. She said I didn't understand. That she left for good reasons."

"Don't be too hard on your mother, Will," Norah said quietly.

"Why shouldn't I be? Aren't you angry with her? What happened between you two? Why did she leave?"

Norah did not answer her grandson's questions directly.

"I am just glad you're here now. Are you up for a walk tomorrow?" she asked.

Chapter Seventeen

1966
RED SLEEVE, WV

Norah and Will

The August sun just crested over the mountain, splashing the stick-strewn path yellow, brightening the trees and rocks from faded to Kodachrome. They'd been walking about an hour, steadily increasing in elevation with every step.

"You okay, Grandma?" Will asked, "do you want to stop and rest?"

"No, if I do I might not get up again," Norah laughed.

"Okay, let me know," he said, wishing she'd take him up on his offer so he could stop and catch his breath. He ran track in school, but his grandmother was in better shape than he was! The wiry, little woman couldn't weigh more than ninety-five pounds soaking wet, but she just kept going. She was tough. Amazing that she lived up here all by herself.

He was so proud to be related to her, to have found her. He was so glad she was still alive to tell him something about himself and his mother. He didn't know what he wanted to know, or why, but he just knew he needed to know it.

He would have to find a way to forgive his mother someday, but right now, he was too angry to even contemplate it. He'd already decided to go straight on to Stanford instead of going back home for a week first. Maybe he would feel ready to talk to her at Christmas. Or maybe he'd just stay out there.

About thirty minutes later, Grandma Norah disappeared.

Panicked, he ran forward along the narrow path. Had she fallen into a hole? Seeing some branches snapping back, he could tell she'd only made a sharp left through some dense brush. Following her, ducking a little to get in, he came out onto the edge of a small, mossy glade, surrounded on three sides by thick forest. On the opposite side, a giant willow arched over the creek, burbling along the far side. It was beautiful . . . and felt very private.

With a smile, his grandmother stepped aside, inviting him in.

"I promise to answer any questions you still have," she said, "but first, let's pay our respects."

Walking past the willow, through a narrow path hidden a few yards away from the stream, she led him up to a small hilly area on higher ground. You couldn't see the creek, but you could hear it murmuring just below.

Will bent down to read the inscriptions on a short row of rounded headstones.

Grandpa McKenna 1849 – 1945

"Grandpa lived to be ninety-seven," Norah said, "least he got to see the war end. We lost so many boys in that war. I know I should feel guilty, but I was glad I had daughters."

Daughters?

Bella

Leila McKenna 1848 – 1930

Giovanni de Mantua 1901 – 1932

Baby McKenna – 1933

Norah patted the ground next to her and Will sat down.

"You keep calling mother Elsie," he said, "My father calls her Ellie, but he's the only one who gets away with it, and only at home. She insists on his using her full name in public, *Eleanor*. Is Elsie a nickname for Eleanor? Did she change her name to spite you for not making Giovanni well?"

"No, Elsie forgived me after a spell. She was just a girl then. Elsie grew up to be a fine young woman, a teacher, just like her teacher said she would. Never made it to Italy, but traveled farther than most do from the holler. Took a job in Cincinnati. Met a fine boy there, married and has three children—two boys and a girl. They used to come and visit, but don't see much of them since the children grow'd up."

None of this made sense. Then Will looked hard at the smallest gravestone. The one that read *Baby McKenna – 1933*.

Norah followed his glance.

"I know these things aren't as important now, but you have to understand things were different then," she said.

"Not long after Giovanni passed, I knew. It didn't matter to me that we'd never married. I was carryin' his child and that child was born of love. That's all that mattered to me."

"When it was time, a woman named Mattie come over from Winslow to help me. Bein' my second, the baby come easier. On the small side, but healthy. A beautiful baby girl."

Will looked confused, but decided to keep listening hoping it would all make sense soon.

"She set to wailin' right off! Mattie washed her up and lay

85

that tiny, pink bundle in my arms. I kissed the top of her little head and put her to nurse, when I seized up and realized another one was comin'. Mattie did her best, but this one was never meant for this world. He was too small and already gone. It was a boy."

Putting his arm awkwardly around his grandmother's thin shoulders, Will said, "I'm sorry." He still didn't see what any of this had to do with his mother.

"Yes, I knew I hadn't had enough to eat that winter, what with grievin' and the Depression gettin' its grip on us even here in the holler. I wasn't the only woman who lost a child that year. Feelin' sorry for myself wasn't going to bring him back—Giovanni or his son.

"I decided to raise this child, his daughter, to be strong. It was 1933. Roosevelt was elected that year. He was a great President. And his wife was a strong woman—a good woman, too. So I gave our daughter her name . . . "

"Eleanor," Will said, the pieces falling into place.

"Yes," Norah said, "Your mother was never a happy child, but she became a strong woman. Always knew her mind. All children hold grudges against their parents, some hold onto 'em longer than others.

"Eleanor's was the shame she felt at havin' no father. No one came out and said it, but she felt the unspoken disapproval of her parents never being married. Always felt people looked down on her.

"Did they?" Will asked.

"Some did, most didn't. Times were changin'. When William David Carmichael II came through here to visit one of his flyin' buddies from the war, Eleanor saw her ticket out. His family was from old money, she'd said. They traced their kin back to Scotland. And accordin' to her, everyone in his family was married and went to church. She was gone before the snow fell that winter."

"Wow," Will said. He never knew how his parents met. His mother referred vaguely to Italian royalty, without coming right out and lying.

"She was a beautiful young woman. I'm sure she still is," Norah said. "I just hope she found what she wanted."

She reached her arm around her grandson and gave him a squeeze, "She had you and you turned out all right."

"But she should be here. Both your daughters should be here taking care of you. Well . . . not here, maybe, but she could fly you to New York, get you an apartment. They have the money!"

"No, I wouldn't fit in no city. I'm part and parcel of this mountain. I'd die in a blink of a gnat's eye if I lived anywheres else. Besides, I didn't raise children to take care of me. I raised 'em to live their own lives."

STANFORD UNIVERSITY
GRADUATION 1969

High noon. Not a shadow in sight.

Seated in the white, plastic, folding chairs in neat rows across the quad, Will hoped the speeches would be short. He was already sweating buckets under his black graduation gown. At least the mortarboards protected his face from the searing sun if he held it at just the right angle.

Will looked around at the campus he'd called home for the last four years. White, roughened stucco walls, red tile roofs baking under a cloudless, blue sky. Pure Spanish mission style. So different from New York.

Earlier, when they were waiting in line to walk in, Sofia had laughed at his complaining. "Feels just like home," she said, closing her eyes and tipping her face to the sun.

From Sicily, by way of Southern California, his fiancée was used to hot summers. He'd better get used to them, too, because after the ceremony they were driving eight hours south to Orange County, CA. Freshly minted aeronautical engineering degree in hand, he'd been offered a job with McDonald Douglas in Huntington Beach, CA. Because the company was a defense contractor, the added bonus was that his new job kept him from having to go to Vietnam.

That made Sofia very happy, but even though he was thrilled to be working in his field, he felt guilty knowing he would be insulated in a suburban house with his wife, while many of his friends sitting here right now would have no protection. In the coming weeks and months, they'd be given a gun, pushed overseas, and dropped directly into the steaming jungles of Vietnam. Several were reporting in the morning.

As the valedictorian wrapped up her comments, he thought of his Grandma Norah, back in West Virginia. He wished she could have been here. He'd offered to buy her a ticket, bring her out, but she said no. That he should save his money, get settled into his job. She invited him to bring his new wife out for a visit next spring, when she could show her the mountains in their Easter finery.

Ceremony over, he looked over the heads of the crowd and found his mother and father standing by the car, waving him over. They were driving to the city. He and Sofia were to meet them at their hotel after they packed up their car, then they'd all go out to dinner.

His parents still made a handsome couple—his father tall and slim with his arm around his mother's shoulders. Her black hair, coiffed perfectly for the occasion, topped by a Jackie Kennedy hat, barely reached his chest. She may be diminutive, but he'd seen her dominate a room many times. He smiled at his mother's outfit—dressed to the nines in a wool suit, nylons, and heels, even in this heat. She'd never quite forgiven him for 'deserting her' by getting and staying in touch with his grandmother, but they'd come to a comfortable truce over the last few years. As long as he didn't mention her, all was well.

Will had to be at his new job next week, so his parents got them all rooms at their hotel—a graduation present of sorts—and they would leave in the morning. Right now they had about three hours to change, pack, turn in their keys and get on the road. The Franciscan was just under an hour away. He dropped Sofia off first, then parked and took the stairs two at a time to his room. His was on the third floor.

Grabbing his suitcase out of the top shelf of his closet, he flipped it open and tossed it on the bed in one move. As he peeled off his damp shirt to put a fresh one on, he noticed a flat, rectangular package on his desk, along with a couple pieces of mail. His mother wouldn't send him a package now, not when she was coming out anyway. She'd have brought it on the plane. And it didn't look like anything his mother would have sent anyway. Wrapped in thick, brown paper, the stiff rectangular box was tied neatly with several strands of rough twine. He finally had to dig out his pocket knife to get it open. There were actually two boxes, with wadded up newspaper as padding in-between. Whoever wrapped this package was determined its contents would arrive undamaged.

Taped to the top of the second box was an envelope with a single sheet of paper inside. It had been typed, then signed in a careful scrawl.

Will,

I am sorry to have to give you such sad news this way, but your grandmother took sick at the start of the year. We never could get her to go to the hospital, but we did get her to talk with the doctor traveling through. Whatever he told her didn't seem to come as any surprise. She seemed at peace with it and passed two days ago.

If it's any comfort to you, we think she died in her sleep. She was very proud of you. Knowing you finished what you started out there made her very happy. She talked about you every chance she got.

Your grandmother was a fine woman. She wanted you to have this. Knowing her time was short, she made me wrap it over three times until she figured it would get to you in one piece.

If your mother is still alive, give her our regards.

Henry

Tears falling on the cardboard box, Will cut the remaining twine and lifted the lid.

Bella.

She'd left him Bella. Wiping his eyes, he saw another note, tucked alongside the violin inside the case. He opened it and read his grandmother's spidery script.

Dear Will,

I know you don't play, but music runs in our blood. Keep Bella safe until that child comes along who will make her sing again.

Much Love,

Grandma Norah

Epilogue

Bella does indeed sing again, in the hands of Logan McKenna. Logan receives her great-grandmother's violin as a gift from her father, Will, when she, like Norah, is drawn to the beautiful instrument and begs to play.

In *Shattered*, the first book in the series, despite being pushed to the back of her closet, literally and figuratively, for years, Bella once again becomes one of the mainstays in Logan's life. She is invited to play at the Otter Arts Festival one summer. Since she's already planning to attend to help her friend, Thomas Delgado, a Native American artist, at his booth there, she accepts.

When a talented young glassblower is found brutally killed at the festival, Thomas is accused of the murder. For reasons of his own, Thomas refuses to defend himself, so it's up to Logan to discover his secret and find the real murderer before they kill again.

Jagged Dawn

Logan's Beginning

To Logan fans new and old—Enjoy!

Chapter One

Friday

Five minutes after exiting the 405 Freeway, Logan McKenna turned right into the first gatehouse after MacArthur and got in line. Normally she just drove in, but her clicker was on the blink. While she waited, she checked out the new sign. Meant to impress, two-foot-high gold letters, precisely and deeply carved into a massive slab of black granite, spelled out *Villa Toscana*, Clarion Group's flagship community. The sign was so huge it could probably be seen from space.

As the attendant waved her in, Logan noticed beads of sweat on his upper lip. She wondered how he could stand this heat. It radiated off the pavement. June gloom with its cool, coastal fog had long since passed, leaving any town more than five miles inland to bake in their Southern-Californian, suburban ovens.

Here in Irvine, where she and Jack had lived since she graduated from UC Irvine (UCI) and had Amy, the ocean was only a few miles away, but it might as well have been a hundred. Other than to visit her dad, Logan hadn't been to the beach in ages.

Once through the gates, a circular drive led residents and visitors through generous, Italian archways and columned terraces. Logan's and Jack's apartment was on the other side of the complex. On her way, she drove past a Junior Olympic salt-water pool and two resort ones. The one good thing about this place as far as Logan was concerned. She loved doing laps in the saline pool after work whenever possible, a great way to unwind and cool off. She left the resort pools to the college crowd.

Each pool area came complete with gas BBQs, flower beds, chaise lounges, scattered tables and chairs, and at least one outdoor fireplace. Across the street there was a steak house too expensive to eat at, a Starbucks, and miscellaneous boutique shops—the kind with fifty-dollar t-shirts prominently displayed on concrete cubes of various heights scattered around an almost empty store. Logan didn't shop there.

For all its luxury surroundings, *Villa Toscana* was lipstick on a pig. Beyond the relaxed, old money, Italian-villa facade, Clarion Group had crammed in over four hundred apartment units. Dubbed in marketing-language as 'Luxury Apartment Homes,' they had the same white paint, cheap fixtures, and scratchy carpet familiar to apartment dwellers everywhere, only the rent was higher. Last week, she'd gotten a notice in the mail that *Villa Toscana* was raising theirs to almost four thousand dollars a month. Logan still couldn't wrap her head around that amount. Their current rent was bad enough— nineteen hundred for a small two-bedroom. By anyone's standards, it was an obscene rent increase.

When she got the notice, she thought it must be a mistake. She'd never heard of anything that draconian. Could they do that?

Yes, Logan was informed by the manager, they could do that. Irvine had no rent control laws. Clarion owned half the city, all of the apartments, and probably a few seats on the city council. The manager said it was out of her hands, and she didn't sound too sorry about it. All financial decisions were made at corporate now. Besides, she'd told Logan, plenty of people from Saudi Arabia and Germany vacationed here and would be happily pay double that price for their Disneyland trips. A couple of Saudi princes already parked their families here full time while they jetted around the world with their mistresses.

The bottom line was that she and Jack needed to pay up or move out at the end of their lease which was, when they got the notice, only two short months away. This from the same people who wouldn't replace the dryer that kept breaking or the perpetually leaking sink.

Jack didn't want to talk about it, but she'd have to find a way to sit him down soon. They needed to make some decisions. Now that Amy was grown and on her own, they didn't really need a two-bedroom. Maybe a one-bedroom would open up somewhere in one of the less luxurious complexes.

They were hardly ever home anyway. Jack was often away on business, and Logan put in long hours at their office, managing the trainers, tech writers, and admin staff as well as handling Jack's ever-morphing travel schedule and client-schmoozing activities. Over the years, she'd managed to line up coveted front-seat tickets to Angels games, Performing Arts Center concerts, and other sports and cultural events. Clients loved Jack. Her husband's expense account was hefty, but then, so were his sales figures. He brought in more business for Primal Concepts Computer Solutions than the rest of the team combined.

What Logan really wanted to do was buy a house. She'd been pushing for that for years, but Jack said they should focus on building the business and not be 'tied down' too soon. They'd been married twenty-plus years. How soon was too soon?

But she had to admit she had a hard time picturing Jack Morgan mowing the lawn after work, or, hammer in hand, catching up on his list of honey-dos on the weekends. Her husband was much more likely to be found at a rugby game with his buddies or taking clients out for dinner. These marathon company meals often took place at Ruth Chris' across the street, complete with twenty-dollar martinis and hundred-dollar steaks. That was one of the selling points of this place for him.

If they couldn't buy a house, Logan wished they could at least rent one in nearby Jasper, CA, the small coastal town where she and her little brother, Rick, had grown up. Their dad, now retired, still lived there. He'd raised the two of them on his own after their mom had left. Dad still lived in the same modest home, and Rick, now a K-9 police officer with the Jasper Police Department, lived nearby. Even Rick had a house. A small one, but still.

Logan sighed, trying not to feel jealous. She knew Jasper was too low-key and relaxed for Jack. She'd learned long ago to pick her battles with her husband. Same with the cars. He insisted he needed the new, top-of-the-line Audi. She countered by driving an old Jeep. It was paid for.

"Cost of doing business, babe!" he always said when she suggested maybe they get something less expensive next time.

When she got to Building C, Logan abruptly turned off the circular drive and plunged from the blinding, summer sun into the belly of the dark, underground parking structure. She'd never quite gotten used it. This part of her day always felt like the beginning of a slasher movie.

Their apartment was on the fourth floor, so it was a good thing there was an elevator. Today, however, the elevator wasn't working. For the third time this year. Hoisting her computer bag onto her shoulder, Logan hiked the four flights of stairs up to a narrow cement walkway. A line of plain doors punctuated the stucco wall on the right. On the left was a stark, iron railing. When Rick came over the first time, he said it looked like a prison, and he wasn't joking. That's exactly what it looked like.

Even if they had a one-bedroom here, she was so over this place. There had to be somewhere else they could live. Maybe she'd have time to look this weekend. Their lease was up in little over a month now, and she sure as hell wasn't going to fork over almost four thousand dollars to the Clarion mafia.

At least the key worked. Logan let herself into the apartment, hung her bag on the peg by the door, kicked off her shoes and went to the kitchen for an ice-cold bottle of sweet tea. Cranking up the air conditioner, she rolled the sweating bottle across her forehead and slumped down in the couch, feet up on the coffee table. She just needed a few minutes. Jack's game didn't start for another hour. She'd take a quick shower, change, and still get there by six. They'd grab some dinner after the game.

Chapter Two

The shower helped. Refreshed and dressed, Logan gathered her purse and keys, then noticed the flowers on the Juliet balcony were wilting. She didn't have much of a green thumb but she couldn't resist picking up a few planter boxes and throwing some color in them just to have something living to look at besides the apartment across the walkway. They were so close, she knew what these people had for breakfast every morning.

She had a few minutes, so hustled into the kitchen. While filling a pot with water, the landline rang. She'd almost forgotten they had one; they hardly ever used it.

"Hello?"

Someone was there—she could hear them breathing.

"Hello?" she tried again.

When no one answered, Logan hung the phone back in the charger, irritated.

Robocall.

She'd been getting a lot of those lately. Usually around this time of day. She'd have to ask one of the techie guys down at the office if there was a good fix for that. She thought she'd gotten on the do-not-call list, but obviously they'd circumvented that, or were just ignoring it.

Throwing enough water on the flowers to keep them from

dying, Logan locked up and was halfway to the useless elevator when her phone beeped. It was Jack, asking her to bring his lucky socks. He never played without them.

Jack's game started in twenty minutes, and it would take her at least that long to get there. Typical Jack. That man had more crises, and most of them self-inflicted. Trying to remember where she'd seen them last, Logan trotted down the stairs to their bedroom and spotted the laundry basket in the minuscule walk-in closet. Pulling it toward her, she emptied it out on the floor and found one sock. Quickly scanning the rest of the pile, she didn't see it. Then she spotted it behind one of his shoes. Reaching for it, she knocked over something leaning on the back wall.

Logan winced. She'd forgotten she'd stashed her violin in here. Checking quickly for damage, she was relieved it was okay. Even though she rarely found time to play it anymore, it was Logan's most valued possession. Not only was it a beautiful instrument, but it was also a family treasure given to her by her father, who'd gotten it from his grandmother. Just touching the case made her long to feel the music resonate through her body as she pulled the bow across the strings. An actual physical need surged through her. Maybe later this weekend, while Jack was still away.

Grabbing the missing sock, she flew back up the stairs, texting as she went.

Got 'em! On my way.

As usual, Jack's team won. Also as usual, Jack was the star player, scoring more points than the rest of his teammates combined. Logan was surprised the other guys didn't complain. Jack was definitely a ball hog, but no one seemed to mind. It was hard to get mad at a guy who was always happy. Logan watched him now, as he laughed and relived the game with the guys over pizza and frequent refills from the frosted pitchers of beer. Compact and naturally fit, her husband was a handsome man. Black hair, black eyes, and a smile full of even, white teeth. Jack wasn't tall or large, but he had the gravitational pull of the sun. Everyone wanted to be in Jack's orbit.

Logan limited herself to one beer, but noticed the guys' pitchers were getting low. Excusing herself, she got up to let the bartender know they needed another round. Before she got there, Jack grabbed her by the waist and pulled her onto his lap.

"You can thank my lovely Logan here for our win, laddies. She brought my lucky socks. Raise your glasses! To the best wife on the planet!"

After accepting her kudos, Logan extricated herself and flagged down the waitress. Jack playfully reached for her, too, but with an experienced sidestep and a smile, the woman smoothly avoided his grab. She'd been at this job long enough to know how to deal with these guys, nimbly straddling that fine line between letting them maul her and losing her tip.

Retreating to the next table, Logan checked her phone for any work emails she needed to answer before tomorrow. Nothing urgent, but there was one from Amy.

Just a few months ago, she and Jack had dropped off their fair-haired, twenty-one-year-old daughter at the airport. Amy was headed to the Africa for a year-long internship as an assistant to a photographer traveling throughout the continent, visiting various tribes, documenting indigenous art and architecture before it was lost.

This was her idealistic daughter's idea of a gap year. Waving a cheerful goodbye was one of the hardest things Logan had ever done, but she'd raised Amy to be independent, and now she had to accept that that independence, in Amy's case anyway, included jumping on a plane to go live amongst the natives, thousands of miles away.

Hi Mom! Sorry I haven't written sooner, but I can only get online in certain places. And before you ask, yes, I'm wearing my sunscreen! Ha, I've got my hat, too. Don't worry. And I'm taking my malaria pills. Don't like them, though. Too much to tell in an email, but the people are all very nice to us. The women make such beautiful things out of nothing. And the huts—they use cow dung to seal the outside and it doesn't smell at all!

Anna says I can keep some of the pictures she doesn't use in the book. I will send when I can. Very hot—they say the desert is spreading because people need to cut down the trees for fuel and stuff—but we have a tent. I am okay. You would love it here, Mom. The sounds at night, the smells in the air. I saw a family of lions! So awesome! Gotta go—will write again soon. Love you bunches!

Amy

Lions?

Logan had to calm her racing heart before answering Amy's email. She strove for a positive, nonchalant tone, as if being within striking range of a wild lions was no big deal. Filling Amy in on her dad's rugby game—Amy never missed a game when she was home—Logan added a funny story Bonnie told her about one of her students, then signed off.

Speak of the devil . . .

Hey Girl, Up for some company tomorrow? I need some pool time! Dying of the heat out here. Thinking of shaving my head to cool off . . .

Bon

Just thinking of Bonnie shaving off her full head of bouncing, blonde curls made Logan laugh. One of her best friends in high school, no one was surprised when head cheerleader Bonnie married hulking rugby forward, Mike. Jack may have been the star Fly-Half, but Mike kept him from getting pounded. Most high schools focused on football, but Jasper's head coach was a former rugby player, a huge Maori from New Zealand, so that's what they played.

Mike, a gentle giant, became a fireman who loved to cook and garden, and Bonnie, who was a kid magnet, became a teacher. It took them a while, but together, they moved to the suburbs and started their own rugby team. Currently, they were up to five. Haley, the oldest, had just turned eleven.

LOL. Can't have you showing up bald when school starts—come on down! I don't have to go into the office tomorrow and Jack is flying up to San Fran for a meeting. Back Monday. Love to have the company. Come anytime. Bring the kids. We can BBQ.
Logan

Lucky you, the kids are in sports camp all week—just us girls! I'll bring the margarita mix . . .
Bonnie

Chapter Three

Saturday Morning

Logan felt good. She dropped Jack off at John Wayne at 6:00 a.m. for an early flight and still managed to fit in her laps before Bonnie arrived. Bonnie claimed to get enough exercise running after her kids, so she was more into stretching out under a palm tree than actually getting in the pool.

Earlier, Logan'd thrown a couple of beach towels over two chaise lounges to reserve them while she came back upstairs to get things ready. She had some hamburger patties in the fridge. They could BBQ those later. Right now, she was cutting up some watermelon and filling a small cooler with ice and bottles of tea and sparkling water. They'd save the margarita mix for later.

As she worked, she looked out across the living room to the open sliding-glass doors. Palm fronds from one of the trees outside framed the balcony doorway. The flowers had perked up after their watering, and it was too early for any noise from pool parties to start blasting, so it was blissfully quiet for a change.

Logan looked forward to catching up with her friend. Normally, Logan worked while Jack was out of town, but she'd just wrapped up an intensive computer-training program with a national optics company. The clients were demanding, but they were one of their major accounts, so she had to play nice. She'd earned the break.

As Logan put the last of the watermelon in the cooler, Bonnie knocked on the open front door frame and bounced in. After five kids, she still looked great. Not as fit as Logan, but Bonnie was one of those people who looked best with a few extra pounds on her frame, most of it in all the right places. She'd always been the curvier of the two.

Today Bonnie sported a cheerful, pink and white, gingham-check, two-piece bathing suit, loosely crocheted white top, and oversized movie star sunglasses. Logan still had on the black one-piece she'd done her laps in, her thick, auburn waves pulled back and more or less secured by a baseball cap.

"Hey!" Logan said, giving her friend a hug. "Almost ready. You need anything before we head down?"

Bonnie reached into one of her many bags and handed Logan a bag of tortilla chips and a Tupperware container with fresh guacamole and lime slices.

"Mike made you your favorite—double jalapeño—just like you like it!"

"Oh yeah!" Logan said, accepting the gift, tucking the guac into the cooler, adding the chips to her beach bag.

Making sure she had her pool key, Logan locked the door and they headed to the pool.

Bonnie's soft curves contrasted with Logan's tall, more athletic frame. As usual, more than one male head turned to admire them walking past.

Several hours later, after the margaritas and burgers, Bonnie talked Logan into extending the day by going down to the Otter Arts Festival in Jasper. Mike said he'd watch the little ones.

Like all the other local kids, Bonnie and Logan had worked at the festival every summer, from when school let out to the end of tourist season in August. Then they had two blessed weeks after the fair closed before school started, to spend their hard-earned summer dollars and have fun.

It was a halcyon time of velvet nights, bonfires at the beach, and living in their bathing suits. Back then, making out meant necking, and smoking was sneaking half a pack of your mom's filtered Virginia Slims. Everything was possible, and the harder world of *OxyContin* and meth had not yet made their debut.

The wildest any of them ever got was when Rick polished off most of a bottle of vodka one night on a bet from his friends. The next morning, when their dad saw Rick's interesting shade of green, he decided to teach him a lesson. No lecture. Dad believed in natural consequences. Dad made Rick get up, do his chores, and go to school *and* his after-school job. No calling in sick. It must have worked. Rick never came home drunk again.

Tonight, though, Logan and Bonnie got to play tourist. Wandering through the jewelry, photography, and pottery booths, they got matching toe rings and big bags of caramel corn, then made their way to the back of the festival grounds to an open area with tree trunk stumps and cafe tables scattered in front of a stage.

"Look! Ned and Sally are playing!" Bonnie said.

An unfamiliar wave of homesickness washed over Logan. She had played with Ned and Sally's bluegrass band at the festival and around town until she graduated from UCI. She always thought she'd continue playing, at least part time, but once she and Jack started the business there just wasn't time.

Ned nodded when he saw them. When their set was over, after picking up their free drinks at the wine bar, he and Sally joined them. Sally's was non-alcoholic. She credited AA meetings and a great sponsor for being twelve years clean and sober.

"Hey, Logan!" Sally said, "So good to see you!"

"How's your sword arm?" Ned asked, "Want to sit in on a set? We've got one more . . . "

"I'd love to," Logan said, "but I'm a little rusty. Haven't played much lately."

She didn't have the heart to tell her friends she hadn't picked up her violin for over a year.

"How's Amy these days? What's she doing this summer?" Sally asked.

"She's in Africa, of all places," Logan said.

"Africa, wow! What's she doing there?" Ned asked.

Logan filled them in, asked after mutual friends around town, and promised to join them onstage next time. No one asked about Jack. Later, when they stopped by to visit with her dad on the way home, Logan noticed he didn't, either. She'd never really thought about it until now, but none of her friends or family from Jasper ever asked about Jack.

Chapter Four

Quillen Financial Services insisted on Logan. Jack had done the initial round of trainings, but Quillen was opening a second division and needed several of their new executives brought up to speed on the new software Primal Concepts had designed. Jack told them Logan was needed to run things back in the office, but they wouldn't close the deal for the second stage of their contract without her.

Logan knew Jack could have handled this training with one hand tied behind his back. He knew their software inside and out. Their programmers had designed it. He'd been here before to do the weeklong initial training. Why they needed two people this time was beyond her, but they were paying well, and it was a short trip. If the company wanted two trainers, they would get two trainers. Logan didn't mind helping out.

So, at ten o'clock Pacific Standard Time, after dropping off their bags at the hotel, she and Jack arrived at Quillen and checked in with the receptionist. The perky young woman recognized Jack from his previous visit and turned herself inside out to escort him 'and his assistant' to the conference room where they could work for the two days they would be in town. Logan didn't bother to correct her.

With his winning grin, Jack offered to help the receptionist get coffee, which she greatly appreciated. She wasn't supposed to leave her desk. Logan started setting up shop.

A few minutes later, a tall, elegant man in a grey suit came in and extended his hand.

"Hello, you must be Logan. Jim Hodges, HR. Thank you for coming. I understand you were needed back in the office, but I appreciate you finding time to make it out."

Logan returned his firm handshake.

"Nice to meet you, Jim, happy to be here," she said. "Jack just stepped out for a minute. I'm sure he'll be right back. We should be ready to start the first session after lunch. We'll get through the basic training this afternoon and tomorrow morning, and still leave time for troubleshooting and individual custom consults in the afternoon. Is one o'clock still a good time to start this afternoon?"

Jim looked over his shoulder into the open office area where Jack was laughing with some people in the break room. He seemed somewhat anxious.

"Yes, the sooner the better, actually," he said. "We'd like to get this wrapped up."

Just then, one of this afternoon's attendees poked her head in the door. It was the office manager's birthday, and they were all going out for a drink after work to celebrate, did Logan and Jack want to join them? They had nothing planned for the evening, so Logan accepted.

Hodges seemed to frown at this suggestion, but maybe she was imagining it.

The session went really well. Logan made sure the computers were shut down and the room secured, then she and Jack took an *Uber* to the bar. Logan nursed a glass of cabernet for an hour or two, but by nine o'clock, she was ready to call it a night. They had to deliver a full day of training tomorrow.

But Jack wasn't ready to go back to the hotel. He'd passed

charming an hour ago and was on his way to sloppy drunk with a hint of mean. At least toward her. Logan had no idea what had gotten into him. She hadn't seen this side of him in a long time. He used to get this way when she did better on a test than he did in Statistics, the one class where her Math/Music classes overlapped with his Business courses, but that was years ago. Not wanting to make a scene, she finally excused herself and went back to the hotel.

Two hours later, Jack still hadn't come home. After calling all the hospitals and checking with the CHP, Logan finally fell asleep around three. He still hadn't called when she left for Quillen the next morning.

At some point, he must have made it back to their room and cleaned himself up. He finally showed up at the training around eleven but sulked in the back of the room while Logan delivered the rest of the class. She was furious but waited 'til they packed up and were back in the hotel room before rounding on him.

"What in the hell?" she said. "What happened last night? Where were you?"

"Oh, don't be so dramatic," Jack said. "It's no big deal. I got a little drunk. I knew you'd be pissed, so I crashed at Bill's place, the guy from accounting. Then I caught a cab back to the hotel this morning."

Logan just glared at him.

"I got there, didn't I?" Jack said.

"Yeah, about three hours late! Why didn't you call? I stayed up half the night worrying about you!" Logan said. "And then I had to go to the client's, make up some excuse for you—told them you were sick—and then put in a full day, acting like nothing was wrong. And then you showed up anyway, which made me look like an idiot!"

"And you did a great job . . . as always . . . Responsible Logan. Efficient Logan. Super-smart Logan!" Jack said. "No one missed me."

Logan had no idea what to say, so she kept her mouth shut. Trying to reason with Jack when he was in this kind of mood was useless. It was so strange, though. What happened to her sweet, funny husband? Something was going on.

Right now, not trusting herself to say another word, she grabbed her bathing suit out of her bag, pushed her feet into some flip flops, and headed down to the pool at the gym to do laps. She could change in the shower. Undressing in front of Jack right now was not going to happen.

They'd deal with this when they got home.

Chapter Five

I t was a long week.

Jack hadn't apologized or explained, but his earlier bluster had faded. He cancelled his upcoming trip and came into the office every day. Logan thought it was almost comical watching him diligently working through his in-basket, returning calls and doing the boring paperwork he usually left for her. He'd tried being charming and flirty, but that hadn't worked. It took a lot to get Logan riled, but once her Irish was up, she didn't back down easily. Jack needed to explain himself.

She kept turning things over in her mind. Had something happened on his previous trip? Had he been drinking? Was that why they insisted she come along this time? Did they think his wife could somehow keep him in line? She had the impression they would have gone with another company if they weren't already under contract to hire them for the second training as well.

She used to do a lot of the out-of-town trainings, but more and more, she did the local ones and Jack did the traveling. Had this happened before? They still had plenty of business, but now that she thought of it, they had lost a couple of clients this year, who hadn't given any particular reason. A knock on the door interrupted her thoughts.

Her handsome husband leaned against the door.

"Hey," Jack said.

Logan was prepared to give him the cold shoulder, but his expression caught her off guard. He looked like he did when he asked her to marry him. Soft. Vulnerable.

"Antonio's?"

Antonio's used to be their favorite restaurant. They hadn't been in ages.

Logan waited. She wasn't going to give in that easily.

"We'll have a nice glass of Chianti," Jack said, " . . . and then we can talk. Okay?"

Logan wanted to make up. She wanted things to be back to normal. She decided to hear him out. She could always get mad again later if the evening didn't work out.

"Okay, but only if Tony's still got his Genoa Triple Lasagna as one of the TGIF specials," Logan said.

A broad grin lit Jack's face.

"Reservation's at seven!" he said. "And I have a surprise!"

Of course, he knew she'd say yes.

○ ○ ○ ○ ○

Antonio's hadn't changed. The rooms were dark, the tables were small, and the line was long. Good thing they had reservations. Jack managed to snag one of the quieter tables by the brick fireplace. Over the Chianti, which was very good, Jack turned on the charm. The real, sincere charm that had won her heart back in high school. He laid his soul bare, said he'd been an idiot. Logan was the best thing that ever happened to him, and could she ever forgive him for being such a jerk? He didn't know what got into him. He had no excuses.

What could she say? This was the father of their child, the only man she'd ever loved. Her husband. She wasn't going to let one incident derail them. Of course she'd forgive him. Like he said, it really wasn't that big a deal. Jack was a good provider. He was faithful. He adored her and always bragged about her to his friends. He was such a fun dad. Amy adored her father. Memories of camping trips and birthdays and holidays all came rushing in.

When Jack leaned across the table to kiss her, she kissed him back.

Jack sat back and let out a sigh of relief which made Logan laugh.

Dessert arrived, and they both dug in. After he polished off the last of his tiramisu, with a look of mischievous, little-boy joy, Jack took a last sip of his espresso and reached into his jacket pocket. He pulled out a Primal Concepts business envelope and slid it across the table.

"Open it!" he said.

"O-k-a-y . . ." Logan said.

This must be Jack's surprise.

Unable to wait for her to finish opening the envelope, he whispered, "New Zealand! For our anniversary!"

Logan's first reaction was *How can we afford this?* but she didn't say this out loud. Instead, she made the appropriate oohs and aaahs at the pictures of the island he had the secretary print out to go with the tickets. They'd just made up, he'd gone to all this effort, and she didn't want to spoil his surprise.

She'd find a way to broach the subject of where the money was coming from later. For now, she allowed her handsome Jack to be the husband who got his wife tickets to New Zealand for their anniversary. He spent the next few minutes gushing about the luxury hotel, the hikes to the glacier, the helicopter ride to the other side of the island and all the other great things they were going to do. It did look great.

Maybe there was a way they could swing it.

While Jack handled the bill, Logan excused herself to use the bathroom. When she came back, he helped her on with her jacket. When they got to the door, a woman Logan didn't recognize stepped in front of them.

"Well, hello there!"

A thirty-something, petite brunette, the woman was dressed in nice slacks and a suit jacket, as if she just came from work. She smiled brightly up at Logan, giving her a penetrating look, then turned to Jack and asked in a bubbly voice.

"Fancy bumping into you here!" she said, lightly touching his arm.

"Rhonda. Rhonda, this is my wife, Logan. Logan, Rhonda," Jack said as the women shook hands. "Rhonda's the regional sales rep for Xerox. She's responsible for the new copier."

Rhonda turned to beam at Logan again. She looked slightly demented.

"Oh, yes, the new copier, it's great—we really needed one," Logan said. "The old one kept jamming."

"One of my best customers, this guy!" Rhonda said, punching Jack's arm. To Jack, she added brightly, "Monday still good?"

"Monday, yeah,' Jack said, "I'll get it set up."

Rhonda stood there a beat too long, giving Logan another searching look, then said her goodbyes.

Outside, temperatures had dropped.

Jack put his arm around Logan's shoulders as they walked to the car.

"Odd duck, that one," Logan said. "Is she always like that? What's happening Monday?"

"Oh, she's coming in to give Jane some training on the advanced features."

Jane was their office manager.

"Since she'll be using the copier the most," Jack said. "And she'll show her how to troubleshoot it when it jams, as it will, at some point."

Yes, Logan reflected, *things always broke.*

Before tucking her into the car, Jack gripped Logan's shoulders and turned her toward him. Holding her at arm's length, he looked directly and deeply into her eyes.

"I love you, Logan," he said. "Don't ever forget that."

Chapter Six

The ride home was quiet. The Audi was in the shop, so they'd taken the Jeep. Jack put on some jazz Logan liked, and she settled back in her seat. It had been a long week. She hadn't realized how tired she was. Leaning her head back, she looked out the window and watched as an ivory moon played hide and seek with some gauzy, coastal clouds. Jack, uncharacteristically silent, reached across and tenderly twirled a lock of her hair around his finger, then ran the back of his hand down her side and squeezed her thigh. Warmth spread through her body at his touch. She slipped her hand into his, absentmindedly rubbing her thumb against his skin.

She missed these moments. She thought they'd have more time together after Amy left, but they'd been so busy. They rarely had time like this to just be, to get back into their feelings, to make love, not just have sex.

Now, there's an idea . . .

Their exit was coming up. Logan closed her eyes and smiled in the dark.

o o o o o

The acrid smell of asphalt filled her nostrils and a stab of bright light almost blinded her. The world was tilted at a forty-five-degree angle. From where she lay, cheek imbedded in gravel, Logan could see people moving back and forth, but she couldn't make out who they were or what they were doing. She tried to move, but only succeeded in sending shooting pain through her neck. After that, she lay very still.

From her limited viewpoint, she could make out a spinning, black tire sticking up from what was left of her Jeep. A few feet above that, a ribbon of twisted metal hung uselessly over the ditch, reaching into dark nothing. The light hurt her eyes, but before she closed them, she saw several firemen working furiously to dig something or someone out from under the Jeep.

A young man materialized beside her, asking her name. He introduced himself as Brad and a young female Logan couldn't see as Peggy. They were going to take care of her. Backlit, she couldn't make out his features. As he checked her over and took her vitals, Peggy relayed the information into a radio of some kind. Probably connected to a hospital. Logan heard bags being torn open and a horrendous, metal screeching in the background, while gentle hands secured a brace around her neck and rolled her onto a stretcher. Lying on her back now, she could only see out of the corner of her left eye, but it looked like the firemen had wrenched one of the doors of the Jeep.

More pain. She managed not to cry out, trying to remember the breathing exercises they gave her when Amy was born. Slow in, slow out.

"You're doing great, Logan, really great. We're going to get you to the hospital now, okay? There's gonna be a little jolt—hang on," the voice said, then louder, talking over her to the person on the other side, "Okay, on three . . . one, two, THREE!"

Searing pain flashed down Logan's spine as they hoisted her into the air. She couldn't help it, a scream ripped out of her.

As they secured her in the ambulance, Logan's mind finally cleared and as Brad flipped the lights and sirens on and pulled onto the freeway, she asked, "Where is my husband? Where's Jack? He was driving—is he okay?"

No one would answer that question, but she saw what looked like another ambulance driving away. Hopefully Jack was in it. She asked Peggy why there were no lights and sirens on it, but the strong, young woman, probably a surfer by the blonde, tan look of her, was busy inserting an IV into her arm and didn't answer. She hung the drip bag, patted Logan's shoulder, and smiled kindly.

"You're going to be feeling a lot better, soon. I promise."

o o o o o

Drifting off into la-la land, Logan remembered almost nothing of the ride to the hospital. The next few hours were a blur of being ferried into various rooms for various tests and getting poked and prodded by a surprisingly large number of doctors and nurses. When they finally wheeled her into a room, the morning sun was streaming in the window. She had visitors.

"Oh my god!" Bonnie said as she rushed over, unable to say more until she hugged Logan, but then stopped when she realized she was hurting her. "Oh, I'm such an idiot. I'm so glad you're okay. Rick called us, and we got here as soon as we could. He went to check with the head nurse to find out when we could see you. I'm sure he'll be right back. He's been barking at everyone for the last two hours . . ."

Logan grinned at the thought. Bonnie continued to fuss over Logan, smoothing her sheets, adding a thick, soft blanket she'd brought in her voluminous bag. It was a soothing, sage green.

"They never have warm enough blankets in hospitals," she said.

Mike, who'd been waiting in the entrance holding a large, bouquet of flowers, came into the room. The nurse got him a vase, and after filling it with water, Bonnie arranged them and put them on the table next to Logan's bed.

Mike pulled a chair over, and Bonnie sat down, taking one of Logan's hands in hers. It took a minute for Logan to ask the question she already knew the answer to.

"Where'd they put Jack? Is he okay? Is he in surgery?"

Bonnie squeezed Logan's hand. "I'm sorry, honey," she said. "I'm so sorry. Jack's not here. He didn't make it."

Logan squeezed her eyes shut—tears leaking out, running down her cheeks—trying to absorb this news. She knew it. Deep down she'd known Jack was dead, but hearing someone say it . . .

"Was anyone else hurt? Any other cars . . ." Logan asked.

"No, Rick talked to the CHP officers, and they said Jack must have swerved to avoid hitting something, or fell asleep at the wheel. They're not sure. Right before the exit, the Jeep ran off the road and hit the guardrail. You were thrown clear. No other cars were hit."

"How did . . . did Jack . . ." Logan stumbled.

Bonnie looked up at Mike before answering Logan's unarticulated question. She knew what Logan wanted to know.

"Rick said when the Jeep rolled, Jack was crushed instantly. He didn't suffer, Logan."

Chapter Seven

The phone call to Amy was the hardest one Logan had ever had to make. All she could do was grip the phone and listen to her daughter sob. Since Amy often worked in remote villages, it had taken almost a week for Logan to reach her at a Doctor's Without Borders station. It took another few days to get her to Nairobi and on a plane home, but Amy was on her way. Her plane landed in twenty minutes.

Against all her doctors' orders, Logan was determined to be there for her daughter when she got off the plane. After signing all her rights away and promising to wear a brace for her lower back, which, it turned out, had sustained more serious injury than her neck, she finally got them to let her out of there.

At two o'clock, they wheeled her to the exit and gingerly loaded her into Bonnie's waiting SUV. She had an L4/L5 herniated disc and some torn ligaments, and the left side of her face still looked like raw hamburger, but she was alive.

Bonnie and Mike had been awesome. During the first few days, when the doctors pretty much kept Logan knocked out with pain meds, Bonnie called everyone who needed to be called—friends, Rick, Logan's dad, everyone at Primal Concepts. Mike notified everyone on the rugby team. Bonnie, the penultimate social organizer, with input from Logan whenever she was able to communicate, made all the arrangements, planned the funeral and got an extension on the apartment lease. The Clarion company gave her thirty days. Thirty days for the death of her husband. And they were going to charge her the higher rent.

Bastards.

The exit for John Wayne, the Orange County Airport, was just one away from where the accident had happened. As they passed the mangled guardrail, Logan shuddered. They'd cleared the accident debris, but she didn't want to look too closely. It all seemed so surreal.

Amy's plane was stuck on the tarmac for an hour, but eventually Logan spotted her coming down the escalator to baggage claim. Her already rail-thin daughter looked like she'd lost twenty pounds and aged a decade in the last week. Amy cried when she saw Logan's face. Logan had forgotten how bad she looked.

Bonnie drove them home but only stayed for a few minutes. She'd come by earlier to make up the beds and stock the refrigerator. After she made them both a mug of hot NightTime tea, she hugged Logan carefully and told Amy to add some slugs of whiskey to their tea to help them sleep. Jack always had some Jameson's somewhere.

Logan and Amy, both exhausted, sat at the kitchen table, taking a few sips of the hot liquid. It burned. Logan didn't mind. She let Amy talk for a while and held her while she cried. But then, knowing Amy would be suffering from jet lag in the morning, Logan insisted they go to bed. They had a long day ahead of them. Amy would need her strength. Tomorrow she'd have to make it through the funeral and then watch as her father was lowered into the ground.

Mike was picking them up at ten. Since the Jeep was totaled, and the Audi was still in the shop, Logan didn't have a car even if she felt up to driving. Neither of them was hungry, but

Logan made Amy nibble a few pieces of toast and have some strong coffee before going downstairs to shower and get ready. Bonnie had thoughtfully purchased a black linen shift for Amy to wear, with a lightweight sweater. Logan wore a simple, navy dress and flats. Jack had preferred her in heels, but there was no way she could walk in those with her back injury.

Dressed and ready, Logan had been up for hours. Pacing herself with the pain medication, she'd taken only half a dose until after the funeral. She planned on knocking herself out tonight after it was all over. Unable to sit for very long at a time, she got up to open the front door. She'd already opened the slider onto the balcony. Maybe she could get a cross breeze going. She much preferred fresh air to air conditioning anyway.

She almost tripped over something on the doorstep. That was weird. UPS usually left packages at the office. But it wasn't a package. It was just a plain shoebox, pink. Her first thought was of a terrorist bomb, then shook her head. Too much TV news.

She lowered herself down carefully, trying not to trigger a back spasm, picked it up, and brought it inside. The lid was sealed shut. Getting some scissors, she cut through the tape and lifted off the lid.

No bomb. At least not the kind that would wound Logan physically. Inside was a stack of papers, bound by a rubber band, some ticket stubs, and a few cocktail napkins. Curious, Logan randomly selected one of the folded papers, opened it, and began to read.

"Mom!"

Logan almost jumped out of her skin! Amy was shouting up the stairs.

"Do you have any deodorant? I forgot to bring mine," she said.

"Top drawer in our bathroom," Logan said.

She almost corrected herself. It was just her bathroom now.

Quickly putting everything back in the box, Logan looked around the room for a good hiding place. A place Amy wouldn't accidentally stumble across it in the next few days.

"Mike will be here any minute, Hon, you almost ready?" Logan said.

"Yeah, almost—be right there!" said Amy.

Logan shoved the box under the couch, way back, then checked to make sure no one could see it from any angle. She'd deal with this later. After Amy left. There was no way she was going to let Amy see the contents. She adored her father. It would destroy her. Anger at whomever left it right there on the doorstep, where Amy could have found it, rose in Logan's breast. But she pushed it down.

Today. She just had to get through today.

Epilogue

Logan packed the last of her now minimal belongings into the Audi, turned in her keys at the office, and drove to her dad's house in Jasper. She gave *Villa Toscana* the finger on her way out. True to their greedy, corporate hearts, the Clarion Group stuck to the one-month extension on their lease, and she'd had to give away or sell everything in their apartment, because storing it would have been ridiculously expensive. The Clarion Group owned most of the storage units, too. What a racket.

Actually, in a weird way, they'd done her a favor. The furniture was all modern, black leather and chrome—more suited to Jack's tastes than hers. And once she got started, there were a lot of possessions she really didn't need or want. The whole process had been cathartic.

Dad had offered to let her stay with him while she apartment hunted, but being a beach town, rates in Jasper were almost as high and few places rented year round. It wasn't likely she'd find anything she could afford there. Bonnie and Mike had offered their mother-in-law unit for as long as she needed it. It had its own entrance. And, it was closer to the office.

Once the funeral was over and Amy was back in Africa, Logan spent the next few weeks really pushing herself in physical therapy. That and lots of ice packs and Jacuzzi soaks helped tremendously. She still hurt, but it was manageable.

Logan was back at work on Monday. She'd called a meeting with some of their key people to share with them where the company was at and how they would move forward from here. She wasn't looking forward to it.

Logan ran the office, but Jack had always kept the books, and in going through the records in preparation for the meeting, she'd discovered what a mess their finances were in. Primal Concepts Computer Solutions was running on empty and had been for some time. She had no idea how she was going to save it, or if she even wanted to.

But that was Monday. The weekend was hers! She looked forward to spending it with her dad. Rick was coming over later, too. It had been just the three of them years ago after their mom left; somehow it felt right to begin her new life here.

Her dad was standing in the driveway when she pulled up, and he was grinning. Logan got out of the Audi and used the key fob to lock the doors. She'd get her roller bag later.

"What's up?" Logan asked. "You look like the cat who swallowed the canary."

In answer, her dad pointed the remote control he was holding in his hand at the garage door.

"Oh my god! Lola!" Logan exclaimed.

A gleaming, sapphire-blue '58 Corvette, Lola was Logan's graduation present from her father. It had been stored in his detached garage out back for years. Jack'd said it was a death trap and wouldn't let her drive it.

"Yep, I know how much you hate that Audi. Thought you might want your own wheels back," her dad said.

It's true that selling the Audi was top of her to-do list. Not only did it remind her of Jack, but less than a year old, it would bring in a good price and infuse her bank account with some much-needed cash.

"She looks great, Dad! What did you do?" Logan asked.

"I hope you don't mind, but with everything else on your plate, I figured I could take care of this. I had Mr. Delgado work on her. He's lightened up the chrome and put in extra power. Fresh paint, new leather interior . . ."

"She's beautiful!" Logan said, running her hand along the smooth body. The chrome scoops on the side shone invitingly.

"Want to take her for a spin?" her dad asked.

"Hell, yeah!" Logan said, getting inside. "Want to ride shotgun?"

"Not this time, Rick'll be here any minute. Just don't drive to San Diego, I'm putting the steaks on at six. Medium rare?"

"With horseradish!" Logan said as she backed out of the driveway.

Mr. Delgado had done an amazing job. Lola ran better than ever and took the curves on Pacific Coast Highway like a champ. For the first time in weeks, Logan felt a thrill of joy rise in her chest. With the sun bathing the coast in golden light, she resisted the urge to keep on going and headed back in time to toss a salad to go with the ribeyes.

For the rest of the night, no one talked about death or funerals, and after Rick went home and she fell into her old bed, Logan slipped into a deep, dreamless sleep. She slept through the night, awaking refreshed for the first time in weeks. Saturday, Rick had to work, but she and her dad went to the farmer's market and then a movie. Ice cream after. Then Mexican food at Juan's.

Sunday morning, after a long beach walk, Logan packed her things into Lola's trunk. It didn't take long. A roller bag, her violin case, some books, and her favorite boots. And in the back, the pink shoebox. She still hadn't decided what, if anything, to do about it. She hadn't opened it again since the day of the funeral.

Leaving the Audi with her dad, who'd offered to sell it for her, Logan waved goodbye, promising to visit soon, and headed to her new, temporary home at Bonnie and Mike's.

Driving south on PCH, Logan luxuriated in the almost empty highway. Checking for cops in the rearview mirror, she pushed the pedal and felt the growling power of the Corvette's beefed up V-8. Cool, ocean air whipped through her hair. Logan licked her lips and tasted salt.

Oh, how I've missed this!

Logan was enjoying herself so much, she drove all the way to San Clemente before finally turning back to take the freeway exit for Bonnie and Mike's home. Reality sunk in as she parked her car in their triple garage.

As lucky as she was to have good friends to stay with until she figured things out, the truth was Logan was homeless, broke, and soon-to-be unemployed. On top of that, her back hurt. Not to mention her heart. The freedom and joy she felt from the infusion of family love and the exhilarating morning ride was fading fast.

But she was a McKenna woman. She'd figure something out.

Want more Logan McKenna?

Read on for a preview of Book 1 in the Logan McKenna
Mystery Series,

SHATTERED

PROLOGUE

The last time she'd seen a dead body, it was Jack's. And it had lain neatly resting in a long, cool coffin, peaceful, far removed from the sights and sounds of death.

Not this one.

Someone had angrily stuffed this one into a white cinder block box—a space much too small for it, like a bundle of human garbage. Neck broken, legs bent like a spider's, jeans drenched in blood, and an almost unrecognizable, bloated, purple-veined face. But she did recognize it, and it belonged to someone much too young to die.

1

AN EVENING EARLY IN MAY

Traces of smoke from distant beach bonfires, mingled with the juxtaposed scents of eucalyptus and jasmine, filled the night. A woodsy aroma rose from the fresh layer of bark chips the groundskeepers had put down earlier in the day. If Southern California had a signature scent, this was it.

Seated on a stool at his workbench in the back, Thomas contemplated his next move. The storage unit he worked in was just an old tent from which they kept the front booth stocked. Canvas walls stretched back about ten feet, supported by a crisscross network of sturdy metal poles. A side flap opened to a warm canyon breeze.

On the rough surface in front of him lay a thin piece of obsidian, measuring a little more than six inches long. It had been carefully knapped, sloping down to a fine edge on either side. The resulting ultra-sharp blade could easily slice through the bones of the hands that made it. Four completed knives lay to his right. A battery-powered work lamp illuminated the area directly in front of him on the table, providing enough light by which to work.

On a narrow shelf just above the obsidian blade lay several curved pieces of antlers ready to be made into knife handles. Elk, not deer. Customers probably wouldn't know the difference if he used deer antler, but he would. The German collector, on the other hand, knew his stuff. He'd insisted on elk.

Thomas considered each piece.

Just as he started to reach for one, his cell phone rang. Placing his materials down on the table, he wiped his hands on his jeans, reached in his pocket, pulled out the phone and answered.

"Hello . . . everything okay?"

Thomas lowered his voice, even though no one else was around.

"Did you get the money?" he asked. "Good."

"Are you sure you can handle this?" he added. "Okay. I just want this to be over."

Thomas ended the call and slid the phone back in his pocket. Satisfied there was nothing more he could do for now, he refocused on his work. Looking over the antler pieces one more time, he reached up and selected one, hefted it briefly and placed it on the table. Holding the long, obsidian blade carefully in the other hand, he held it against one end and then the other of the future handle, trying to decide which angle worked best.

He loved working at night. No interruptions or customers asking questions. The quiet was deep but something made him stop, sit up, and listen. Pinpricks ran up his spine. He rubbed the back of his neck and shook it off. Probably nothing.

Still.

Turning slowly, he looked over his left shoulder. He was not alone.

One of the young glassblowers, Elizabeth, leaned coolly against the metal post in the doorway formed by the open flap, arms folded. Not a hair out of place, her thin ponytail cut a perfect, white-blond scythe out of the soft, night sky. Oozing confidence, her face looked deceptively delicate in the residual light from the lamp. It also looked smug.

You only had to meet Elizabeth once to know she was trouble. Keeping a tight lid on his mouth and his emotions, Thomas wondered how much she had heard.

"Sounds very hush, hush, Thomas. Keeping secrets from the wife? Gambling? Get someone pregnant?" Elizabeth fished, her blue eyes glittering like tiny chunks of Arctic ice.

Thomas decided to wait her out.

When he neither denied nor confirmed, she continued, strolling into the tent, "What's the money for? Let me guess . . . an abortion? Something worse?"

Thomas crossed his arms and leaned back on the counter, quickly calculating the damage and what he could do about it, careful not to let his face betray his mounting concern. Whichever way this went down, he would protect Lisa. Of that one thing, he was very sure.

Elizabeth paused, looked down at her feet, and straightened her shoulders. With something bordering on an apology she looked directly into his eyes.

"This isn't personal, Thomas. I didn't plan to overhear your conversation tonight. But I've learned to take luck where I find it.

"So, I don't know who you paid to do what, but as long as you're writing checks, you can send some my way. $8,000 ought to do it."

She waited to see if this amount would fly. Thomas didn't object, so she continued.

"I need airfare for the competition, and I'm short some to set up my own studio. When I get back, whether I win or not, I'm going solo. I'm tired of dealing with troglodytes like Matt."

She almost spit out the name. Elizabeth squinted at him, waiting to determine the efficacy of her threat.

Thomas wasn't sure what she was capable of, but she looked dead serious. He'd only met her once before, when he was out visiting Howard at his compound where he and his interns lived and Howard gave classes. She'd half-heartedly hit on him. He'd politely, but firmly, made it clear he was married and that had been the end of it. In fact, he thought she was seeing Matt, one of the other glassblowers, but after what she'd just said, that didn't seem likely. He hoped she wasn't the type to hold a grudge.

Apparently that had nothing to do with it, because she didn't act like a woman scorned, just one on a mission, and after overhearing his conversation, an opportunity to fulfill it—with his money.

Thomas had about $20,000 in the bank. He'd just gotten a large order from his German collector. That's why he was working so hard now, he had to replace his inventory before the festival. Luckily, Elizabeth didn't know this or she'd have asked for more.

$10,000 was already going to the man on the phone, so $8,000 was doable. Adopting Elizabeth's pragmatic attitude, he went to the bank in the morning and withdrew that amount. It was from his business account, which Lisa never checked. Until recently, it wouldn't have been worth it if she did, as the balance rarely rose above $150. If she ever discovered the missing money, he would just have to explain what it was for. Money meant nothing. He'd do anything to protect his wife.

Read the full story in
***Shattered*: A Logan McKenna Mystery Book 1.**

Acknowledgments

Every writer owes a debt to all those experts who share their knowledge generously with us. Without them, we could not offer authentic details to our readers for all the professions, geographical locations, flora, fauna, and historical context in which our stories are set.

For Bella in particular, I owe a debt of gratitude to many because it is set in places and times with which I had limited experience.

First, thanks go to Tom Olsen of Guild of American Luthiers, for his expertise in the making of violins in general, and in Appalachia, specifically. Without him, Giovanni would not have been able to craft Bella for Norah with the materials available to him in West Virginia, nor known which items he would have to bring with him from Italy.

There are too many sites to name, but as always, I appreciate the miraculous and under-appreciated resource that the internet proves to be over and over again for authors. Thanks to the many websites that provided in-depth information about life in coal mining towns, and the very real struggles to unionize that were finally successful in 1933. People take for granted our forty-hour workweek, weekends off, and safety regulations that were only dreams before unions were formed. Gallville and Red Sleeve, WV are entirely fictitious, while Matewan, WV exists.

The wealth of information available about Ellis Island is fascinating and gave me an idea what a typical Italian immigrant at that time would experience on their arrival.

When I was a girl we lived in Italy for several years and I fell in love with the country. However, we lived in Livorno, near Genoa, Italy, so I relied heavily on university and historical sites to envision Giovanni's hometown of Mantua and the process of violin-making at that time. I also lived in Virginia for four years between fourth and seventh grades. I pulled from the rich, natural beauty of those areas, particularly the creek that ran along the back of our property and the dogwood tree bursting with blossoms in the spring. I remember spending as much time exploring my new world as possible, squishing my toes in the mud.

A huge debt is owed to the Foxfire books, which I fell in love with while working in a bookstore in Utah in 1973. What began as a school project in Appalachia—where students went into the hills to gather wisdom from the old people before it was lost—turned into at least four books that I know of, each filled with knowledge of how to build a log cabin, render a hog, and make soap, quilts, cane baskets, and home remedies. Foxfire books are out of print, but I recently found a set online and snapped them up.

As a starry-eyed eighteen-year-old, I was all set to go homestead in Idaho, or Wyoming, or anywhere that would take me, all because of the those books. They were probably a large part of why I selected a major in Cultural Anthropology and enjoyed collecting the life histories of Vietnamese refugees. I remember taking a genealogy class once and our first assignment was to contact the oldest living member of our families. They had stories and wisdom we needed to write down before they died. Still true today.

I particularly enjoyed watching Praise to the Hand, a black and white documentary about violin making, sans dialogue, production by Zagreb film, 1968.

Big hugs and huge thanks to my faithful Alpha and Beta Readers, who help streamline and strengthen the story before it goes to the editor. And speaking of editors, I was lucky to find Kimberly Peticolas. Recommended by several fellow authors, she's knowledgeable and a joy to work with. (And yes, Kim, I know that sentence ends with a preposition . . . I just wanted to drive you crazy!)

As always, my deepest thanks go to my husband and family, who always have my back, along with strong coffee and kudos. You keep me going, guys!

Enjoyed the Book?

I f you enjoyed this book, please consider leaving a review on Amazon or Goodreads. And be sure to check out the rest of the Logan McKenna series.

SHATTERED: Logan Book 1
FOREST PARK: Logan Book 2
DEVIL'S CLAW: Logan Book 3
VANISHING DAY: Logan Book 4
SAFE HARBOR: Logan Book 5
LIES THAT BIND: Logan Book 6 (Forthcoming)

Want to know more about Valerie Davisson or her next book? Make sure to visit www.valeriedavisson.com and sign up for her newsletter.

More from Valerie Davisson

NON-FICTION
SATURDAY SALON: Bringing Conversation & Community Back Into Our Lives

POETRY
Tilting Windmills I

About the Author

A self-admitted book addict, Valerie Davisson was the kid with the flashlight under her pillow, reading long after lights out. After a life of travel, she now lives on the Oregon coast with her husband, John, and their new puppy, Finn. When not working on her latest book, she's probably in the kitchen, cooking up a storm for family and friends.

Made in the USA
Middletown, DE
29 August 2020

15567959R00086